Murder Hosts an Event

Murder Hosts an Event

Shannon Symonds

SWEETWATER BOOKS
An imprint of Cedar Fort, Inc.
Springville, Utah

ISBN 13: 978-1-4621-4080-0

Published by Sweetwater Books, an imprint of Cedar Fort, Inc.
2373 W. 700 S., Springville, UT 84663
Distributed by Cedar Fort, Inc., www.cedarfort.com

Library of Congress Control Number: 2022933518

Cover design by Shawnda T. Craig
Cover design © 2022 Cedar Fort, Inc.
Edited and typeset by Valene Wood

Printed in the United States of America

10 9 8 7 6 5 4 3 2 1

Printed on acid-free paper

For the children of Lassie Hame.

Thank you for walking with me on my author journey and setting some of the most epic bonfires the Oregon Coast has ever seen!

Other books by Shannon Symonds

Safe House
Finding Hope

The By the Sea Cozy Mystery Series

Murder Takes a Selfie
Murder Makes a Vlog
Murder Has a Ball

Contents

Chapter One

Invited to Mind the Fish

A pebble flew through Esther's open bedroom window and bounced across her desk at the same time as her alarm chimed for school. When she rolled over to turn it off, her cat, Miss Molly, slid off her back. It was five thirty in the morning. Another pebble skittered across the desk and bounced on the hardwood floors of her third-story bedroom in the James family home by the sea. A slow smile spread across Esther's face. Molly stretched and Esther slid out of bed and leaned across the desk at the open window to see Sophie, her best friend, waving in the morning light.

"Open up!" Sophie was trying to talk quietly, but her voice carried all the way to Esther's window in the round turret of her Queen Anne Victorian house. Sophie picked up a full laundry basket and walked toward the front porch.

Esther quickly put on her glasses and pulled her favorite hoodie over her t-shirt and flannel pajama bottoms before she headed downstairs to let Sophie in. Her bare feet padded along the hall past Mary's room, the bathroom, and Mom and Papa J's room before she took the stairs at a run, crossed the spacious living room, slid on the entryway rug, and slammed into the front door.

Esther opened the door. "Hey. Did you run away from home? What's with all the things?"

Sophie snickered softly. "Are you kidding? You should run away and live with me. My house has the biggest television in town and a bank of computers. You could run Homeland Security from my basement. The basket has my necessary stuff: my laptop, fish, and things that wouldn't all fit in my backpack or my dinky suitcase. Hold the door, the basket is heavy."

Holding the screen door open, Esther let her in to the quiet house. Sophie was already dressed for school in her favorite plaid skirt and black cardigan, buttoned to the top. She dropped the basket onto the couch by the fireplace. The water in the fishbowl sloshed. She picked up the bowl and examined her fish, whose name was The Angel of Death, because he ate all the other fish in the tank.

After giving Esther the fishbowl, Sophie used both hands to push up her round black glasses before she slipped out of her backpack and put it next to the basket. "Mom and Dad just left for the airport. They didn't take Spam, so I'll have to walk and water him in the morning and evening. He has a doggy door and his own little doggy yard, but he gets lonely."

"Where are they going?"

"You know the Silver Pearls—the group that my grandma belongs to in Hawaii? The old ladies that go snorkeling, rock climbing, and wakeboarding together? Apparently, they tried something new, ocean kayaking. Grandma bought one and everything. Well, one of the members accidentally hit grandma with her paddle pretty hard. She went overboard and hurt her knee on the rocks."

"Ouch. Is she okay?"

"She's going to need surgery, so Mom and Dad are flying to Oahu to help her out. They called your mom last night. She said you would adopt me for a few weeks."

"Perfect! We can get to work on scholarship forms and make a college dream list."

"Whoa. Hold back." Sophie put her fish on the fireplace mantle. "Don't go wild on me, E. Can I plug in the fish tank filter here?"

Esther chuckled. "Sure. Do you want to take your stuff upstairs, or do you want to eat?"

"Are you kidding me? Food, of course. I don't want to carry this stuff another five feet."

The fridge was packed. Esther moved things around while Sophie looked in the pantry.

"There's nothing to eat." Esther shut the refrigerator.

"I know." Sophie pulled out a box of granola. "Is your mom on a health food kick?"

"Don't get me started. Do you want some Greek yogurt with that?"

"Sure."

Esther gathered the yogurt, a basket of fresh strawberries, and two diet soda pops. "Breakfast of champions. Oh look, I found bacon."

"See, you should stay with me. We have Toaster Tarts." Sophie got out the bowls and spoons.

"You have all the good stuff." After Esther used a hair holder from her pocket to tame her messy brown curls, she rinsed the berries and sliced them over bowls of yogurt and granola.

"Hey, did you get an invite to that one weird event?" Sophie put a cast-iron skillet on the large gas stove and opened the bacon.

"You mean the one online?"

"Yeah, that one."

"The one with a photo of Madison's new amphitheater and park?"

"What did you think?" Sophie asked.

"I thought it was seriously creepy. You're invited to *The End* is all it says, besides the date and time."

"What you guys doing?" Esther's seven-year-old sister, Mary, stood in the kitchen doorway in her favorite rainbow unicorn onesie pajamas. She had the hood up, but her silver horn drooped to one side. She pointed at them with her glitter wand.

"Nothing, your royal highness." Esther roller her eyes at Sophie. Esther loved Mary, but as a little sister, she could be pretty demanding.

"I want bacon and marshmallow cereal. So does my friend, Amy." Mary sat down at the long wooden table in front of the fireplace.

"Amy? Who is Amy?" Esther's crooked smile made a single dimple pop on her left cheek.

"Amy is my imaginary friend," Mary said. "You have Sophie Eats and I have Amy. Amy likes to eat too."

"What does Amy want to drink with her bacon?" Sophie asked. She pretended to hug Amy.

"Amy likes kisses." Mary tapped her chin and thought for a minute while Sophie kissed imaginary Amy.

"Orange soda." Mary waved her wand. "Bring us orange soda."

"Mary, you know I would get in trouble if I gave you sugary soda before school," Esther said.

"You're drinking some." Mary pointed at Esther's soda with the glitter wand, waving the ribbons tied to the end back and forth.

Esther sighed heavily. "It's diet. How about orange juice or grape juice?"

"Grape and cereal."

"Alright, little miss Mary." She poured the grape juice. "Sophie, do you think anyone will go to the event?"

"Go where? Amy wants to go." Mary sat up, excited at the prospect of going anywhere.

"The event isn't for you or your friend, Shorty," Sophie said. The bacon sizzled as she turned it with a fork. "I think I might go—just to see what it is."

"I was wondering if Madison Merriweather is hosting the event to launch her next book. We should ask Bridget," Esther said.

Sophie put a piece of bacon on a plate. "What do you think of Madison's amphitheater, The Stone Circle?"

"I haven't been up to see it yet, but the photos make it look amazing."

The door to Esther's Grandma Mable's apartment on the back of the house opened and Nephi, her seventeen-year-old uncle, came into the kitchen, barefoot, in shorts, and right out of bed.

Esther loved Nephi like a best friend. They had been through a lot together since she began dating his buddy, Parker. He looked like an arrogant athlete, a popular girl magnet, but Esther knew his good looks often masked surprising wisdom. She also knew from experience that he would be there for her through the worst moments life threw at her while he laughed inappropriately at all the wrong times.

His normally perfect hair stuck up on one side. He scratched his belly under his torn t shirt. "Do I smell bacon?"

"You smell like something. Go back to bed. We don't have enough," Sophie said. She smiled and tried to swat his hand away from the plate. The more Sophie teased Nephi, the more Esther suspected Sophie likes him.

Laughing, Nephi ignored her and took the one she had off the plate and chewed on it.

"Hey," Mary whined. "That was my imaginary friend Amy's bacon."

"Wait your turn, Amy," Esther said.

"Who is Amy?" Nephi asked.

"My friend. Can't you see her? She's my imaginary friend," Mary said.

"Then she can eat imaginary bacon." Nephi smiled and sat by Mary.

"You're sitting on Amy," Mary said. Nephi kissed her head and she smiled back. Mary adored Nephi. He could get away with squishing Amy and anything else in Mary's world.

Esther gave Mary a bowl of cereal. "Anyway, I think the amphitheater is beautiful. But the event gave me the shivers. Maybe it's just the black-and-white photo of the stone circle with an ocean storm behind it."

"We need to go see the new park." Sophie put the rest of the bacon on the plate and turned the stove off. "Do you think the cement Stonehenge is authentically sized? I've always wanted to see the real one."

Nephi sat at the table with a large glass of orange juice. "Stonehenge is cool. We should all go. I'm guessing the event is just another party set up by someone at school. And I was invited because they want me to go. Everyone wants me."

"You're wanted alright. Get your feet off the table." Esther pushed them off.

"Do you know what else is creepy, besides you?" Sophie said. She pointed at Nephi with her spoon. "Your new neighbor."

"Right?" Nephi sat straight up. "Did you know he has like a thousand cats?"

"Four. He has four," Esther corrected him.

"I don't know how many cats he has," Sophie said. "But he was sitting in the dark on his porch when I passed his house this morning, petting one. I wouldn't have even seen him at all, except the cat was purring." Sophie shivered. "Creepy is the right word."

"I think he has some weird crush on Grandma Mable," Esther said.

"What makes you think that?" Sophie asked.

"Gross!" Nephi got up and put a bagel in the toaster.

"Grandma's a fox. Yesterday, he was leaning over the fence and waved wildly when she left for the grocery store." Esther tipped her head and looked knowingly at Nephi.

"So, he waved at her," Nephi said.

"Hey?" Sophie said. "What's wrong with liking Mable? I love her. Your mom can take care of herself. She's old Army. She worked with the M.P.s before women were allowed to. You should be more worried about what she could do to Marion," Sophie said.

"That's just gross." He grimaced.

Mary folded her arms. "I'm telling Mom." And with that, she ran for the stairs.

"Great. Now you've done it." Nephi laughed. "I guess I should go take a shower." He popped the bagel from the toaster and ran for the door.

"Coward!" Sophie called after him.

Chapter Two

Mable's Meet Up

Esther and Sophie sat on the porch swing, waiting for Nephi. The morning light shone through white clouds that floated at ground level, revealing the neighborhood in random pieces. Absentmindedly, Esther pushed the swing back and forth with her toes, knowing Sophie was too short to reach the deck of the large wraparound porch. The sun began to dissolve the clouds and gradually the grayish white morning became bright with blue skies.

Sophie sat up. "Did you answer the letter from your dad? Are you okay with all the letters your dad keeps sending from prison?"

"Sort of. I haven't really answered them. He keeps asking about school and what I'm doing. Dumb stuff. What do you say to the person that abused your mom, tried to kidnap you, and then asks you to forgive him? Seriously. Sometimes, I just want to tell him and the drama that follows him to go away."

"I don't blame you." They rocked silently for a moment. "Nephi's going to make us late." Sophie sighed and pulled her long black ponytail tighter.

Esther smiled. "You're not surprised, are you? It takes a long time to shake the wrinkles out of his face and flat iron his hair. You don't think he smells that way naturally?"

"He smells great."

One of Esther's brows involuntarily rose as she looked at Sophie who looked back and shrugged, giving her a cheesy grin. The wooden front door opened, and the screen door slammed. Nephi stepped out without any books. He was wearing a white hoodie, jeans, and flip flops. His hair was controlled by product, which also held a number two pencil in place over his left ear.

"Let's roll." He took the stairs two at a time and jogged across the dewy lawn to his beat-up truck.

Sophie stood up and sniffed.

"It's like a wake of man perfume," Esther said.

"Yes, it is."

Esther could see that Nephi was turning the key in the ignition, but nothing was happening. He pounded the wheel and said something she couldn't quite understand. When he got out of the truck, he slammed the door and leaned against it with his arms folded and his mouth in a firm line.

Nephi looked at the girls, "It won't start."

"We can't be late," Sophie said. "The school board meeting is today and since we work in the library, we said we'd help set up."

"Chill. I'm calling for backup." He took his phone out of his back pocket. "Hello, Mom? The truck won't start . . . thanks."

They all leaned side by side on the truck, looking at the new neighbor's house.

"Did he rip all of Mrs. Anderson's rose bushes and her entire lawn out?" Esther asked.

"It looks like a giant kitty litter box." Sophie pointed to a cat sitting on top of a pile of sand.

"Hello!" The neighbor came down his steps in a red silk robe, sweatpants, and slippers, holding a cat in his arms. The cat was the same color as his chest hair, medium brown, and stood out against the robe. So did the dozens of other cat hairs stuck to his velvet lapel.

The neighbor smiled. "I don't think we've had a chance to meet yet. I'm Marion Joseph Herbert and this is Anni-Frid. Do you kids need a lift to school?" He stroked the cat, who growled at Nephi.

Esther didn't know what to say. It was clear Nephi wasn't going to talk, and she was afraid Sophie would. Finally, she said, "We noticed you have a lot of cats."

He giggled. "Oh, not so many. Just four, Anni-Frid, Benny, Bjorn, and Agnetha. Isn't she beautiful?"

"Wait. Aren't those the names of the members of the band called Abba?" Sophie eyed him and pushed her round glasses up her nose.

"Are you an Abba fan too? I absolutely adore their music."

"My parents are. They like classic rock."

"Classic?" He threw his head back and laughed. "I guess that makes me a classic too." Then his eyes lit up, and his mouth fell open.

Esther followed his gaze to the front porch, and Grandma Mable. Her red hair was on fire with flecks of gray, like a lit match in the morning sun. A seagull called and landed on the roof of the porch.

Mable looked up. "Shoo, bird. You're not getting me today."

Esther looked back at Marion. He was still staring at Grandma Mable and petting his cat. His eyes were fixed on her.

Grandma Mable shook the keys to the Jeep. "All aboard." She started down the steps.

Then Marion strode past Esther. He struck a pose between Mable and the SUV. "Hello. I just had to come and introduce myself. I am Marion. Marion Joseph Herbert. I just bought the house next door."

"I know. You destroyed the one-hundred-year-old rose bushes. I would have come over and transplanted them for you, you know." Mable folded her arms. "Kids, get in the car."

"Oh, dear. I had no idea they were that old. I didn't destroy them. I actually donated them to the men's shelter on the Washington Peninsula."

"That's a relief. You better call them and tell them what they have. Those were grown from a cutting from the Captain's Cove Mansion."

"Really?" Marion stepped back and put his hand over his heart. "Now I wish I hadn't pulled them out."

"What are your plans for the moonscape?" Mable asked.

Marion chuckled and beamed. "I thought I would bring a little bit of the Arizona desert with me. I am putting in a beautiful rock garden. They're low maintenance."

Mable didn't flinch. Her face never changed. "Are you retired?"

"Oh, not even close. I am a licensed clinical social worker. I am working on getting everything in order to do couples counseling in that beautiful space over the carriage house I use as a garage."

Mable's gaze shifted to the three-story carriage house. Esther studied her face. But if Mable had any emotions, she wasn't sharing them.

"I hope you don't mind. I will only be holding sessions during the workday, and quarterly weekend retreats. I promise to make sure parking doesn't become an issue. The city already cleared my zoning."

Mable had done it. Esther had experienced it a thousand times. She would stand silently until you found yourself blathering on about every little thing you never wanted to tell her.

"Mom. We're going to be late." Nephi stood at the car door with Sophie. "It's locked."

"Excuse me, Marion. It was nice to meet you."

"The pleasure is all mine." His shoulders relaxed and he waved enthusiastically as they pulled away from the curb.

"He is so weird." Esther leaned toward the front seat. "Did you hear him? His cats are named after the members of a band?"

Nephi, who was sitting next to Mable, took a piece of gum from the glove box. "I think he likes you."

Mable didn't flinch. "Haven't you all learned anything about judging people?

Sophie cleared her throat. "In today's world, it behooves us to determine if the adults operating in proximity of our personal space are safe and trustworthy. We're practicing skills that will be extremely useful when we manage fortune five hundred companies."

Mable finally lost her composure and cackled. "We shall see, Sophie. We shall see."

The drop-off lane moved slowly. Madison Merriweather's Range Rover was ahead of them by a car length. When it was her turn in the Oceanside High School Roundabout, she parked.

"Only Madison would park." Nephi chuckled and shook his head. "Become a world-famous author and they stop yelling at you in the drop-off zone."

Sophie leaned forward. "Maybe she didn't get the eighteen-point pickup and drop-off zone red letter in the orientation packet. Whoa. Look at her."

"Who is that?" Nephi put his head out the window to get a better look.

Madison had changed. She wore black sweatpants which accented her muscular legs. And she had on tennis shoes instead of her usual heels. For the first time in Esther's memory, her hair was up in a ponytail. She still had on her typical layers of jewelry, but Esther had never seen her in workout gear and tennis shoes. In fact, she had rarely seen her without a large coffee or drink in her hand.

"Those are some expensive shoes." Nephi whistled.

Madison's head snapped around and he ducked back in the truck. She smiled and waved. He weakly waved back. Esther couldn't help it, she started laughing at him.

Sophie gave him a friendly push. "Seriously? We can walk from here. See you, Grandma Mable."

The girls were still giggling when they shut the car door and waved goodbye. Esther's phone chimed twice. She pulled it out of her pocket.

Text from Parker. *Lunch together today?*

Text from Esther. *Yes, please!*

Esther waved at Bridget and called her name. Bridget waved back and walked toward them.

"Oh, no. Mrs. Boxer is coming for Madison," Sophie said. An intimidating woman in an orange traffic vest and matching hard hat was marching towards Madison, waving a hand-held stop sign with a whistle dangling from her lips.

"You can't park there! Move it!" Mrs. Boxer yelled after blowing her whistle.

Madison looked surprised and pointed at herself. "Me?"

"That's right! Don't you know the rules?"

"Rules?"

"Move it!"

"It's just for a moment." Madison raised her eyebrows and held her hands out. "Please?"

"Move it or I will!"

Esther heard a car honk but couldn't figure out who the rude culprit was. Madison shrugged and hugged Bridget, whose face was now bright red. She got back in her car and the drop-off line slowly inched forward again.

Bridget, Esther, and Sophie walked together up the stone steps to Oceanside High School.

"Your mom looks great," Esther said.

"Yeah. What happened to her?" Sophie asked.

Esther elbowed Sophie. "Sophie!"

Bridget smiled. "It's okay. I'm not sure. About two months ago, Mom said Parker and Paisley's mom, Mrs. Stuart, was doing this life coach thing that came with workouts. I guess Mrs. Stuart is studying to be a personal trainer or nutritional life coach. Something like that. She asked Mom to workout with her."

"What kind of diet are they on?" Esther asked.

"Well, that's the problem. She is so into it. She thinks we should be on it together. She says it isn't a diet. It's a lifestyle change. But I am dying. It's a lot of whole organic foods, no sugar, and these horrible green shakes that she adds spinach to."

"That's disgusting," Sophie said.

Esther pushed the heavy front door open and held it for Bridget and Sophie. "I think my mom is on the same diet. She stopped buying anything that tastes good, and she has a massive new blender."

Sophie's eyes opened wide. "Crepes! You mean I'm staying with you, and your mom isn't going to make popcorn or cookies? I'm going to starve to death. What happens if I need fries and a burger? What if I want ice cream infused with an extra megadose of chocolate syrup?"

Bridget laughed. "You're right. Your mom joined the group. She was at Mrs. Stuart's Power Meeting. My mom made me go."

"Why do you have to go? You're already healthy," Esther said.

"She calls it our bonding opportunity. She thinks I am growing up too fast, and she is going to be alone soon. I have to spend more quality time with her before it's too late." Bridget listed her mother's reasons in a monotone voice, like a rehearsed script, and rolled her eyes.

"It's not like you're going to die or something when you get out of school," Sophie said.

"Right?" Bridget said. "That's why she is coming in today. You know the park she's contributing to the city? She has this hairbrained idea for launching her next book there and wants me to be center stage with her."

"I knew it." Esther gave Bridget a broad smile, with white teeth and both dimples. "I love it when I'm right, just like Sherlock Holmes."

"Or Shaggy and his dog," Sophie said.

Just as the bell rang for class, someone grabbed Esther's arm and pulled her around.

"Parker!" Every part of her face smiled.

"Good morning." He gave her a hug. "I can't be late. Meet me at the library for lunch? My treat? Sophie and Bridget, you come too?"

"Burgers?" Sophie asked.

"Whatever you want. We're celebrating."

"What are we celebrating? Esther asked.

"It's a surprise. Gotta go. I can't be late." Parker and Bridget melted into the steady stream of students, leaving Sophie and Esther to walk to the library on the west side of the old school. Lockers slammed, kids scattered, and the last bell rang, leaving behind a piece of paper floating to the linoleum floor.

Esther and Sophie had so many credits in their junior year, they were allowed to take a study period and library sciences for several hours a day. The beautiful library was the heart of the school for Esther. It was their sanctuary and the place where she'd first talked to Parker and gathered with their friends.

The Oceanside High Library was the only place she felt truly safe. In between the shelves and among the books, everything was predictable, quiet, organized, and so unlike the fights of her early childhood. By opening a book, she could run away from high school drama in the library. In this place, the librarian, Miss Priest, and Sophie understood her. She could open any volume and escape into another world where people like her, invisible, introverted, observers became heroes. She had read every *Agatha Christie* novel and loved the little-old-lady who outwitted the police. When she was still Mary's age, she was already consuming *Nancy Drew* novels. When no one was looking, she would open a book and just breath in the scent.

The wooden doors to the library were beautifully carved by some unknown workman in the 1800s. The ancient, hand-blown glass was still wavy and pitted. Not far into the spacious two-story library was the front desk. It was carved to match the door. But something was different.

"Hello. What's this?" Sophie said. She reached out and touched a new tablet on a stand.

"Good morning," Ms. Cynommon Priest called from her office. "Do you like our latest edition?"

Esther put her backpack under the counter and hung up her hoodie on the coatrack behind the desk, silenced her phone, and stuffed it in the back pocket of her jeans. "I don't know . . . Do we still get to use my favorite date stamp and ink pad?

Ms. Priest laughed lightly. "If you want." She joined the girls.

"Nice dress," Sophie said. "What's the occasion?"

She smiled and bowed in her black jumper and matching jacket. "Thank you. The school board meets here today, remember?"

"Do we get to use the tablet to check out books? Does it come with a barcode scanner?" Sophie asked.

"We'll be gradually including a bar code system for loaning books, which should speed things up. It's been in the school budget for two years. They finally agreed to go forward as long as I have you two to help me prep all the books and get the system running. They might even give us one more student aide to work on the project. If you're game, we'll all get trained next month. It's a big undertaking. We won't have it fully rolled out until the end of summer."

"That slaps!" Sophie said.

"Excuse me?" Cynommon cocked her head and raised her brows. "Slaps?"

"She's trying not to food swear so much. I encouraged her to read the urban dictionary and collect more slang." Esther grinned from ear to ear.

"So, what does it mean?" Ms. Priest said.

"It's awesome. The bomb. You know?" Sophie said.

"No. But I see Madison Merriweather is on the way in. You'll have to bring me up to speed later." Miss Priest smiled and left them to meet Madison Merriweather at the door.

The west doors opened, and Madison, their friend Bridget's mother, their new friend, and passionate school board member, made her usual grand entrance. "Hello, my lovelies!" Arms open wide and a joyful grin on her face, eyes twinkling, she gave them each a perfumed hug. "I had to come in and invite you all to workout with us tonight. We're having so much fun, you simply must join."

"Is that the class Bridget was telling us about? Parker and Paisley's mom, Mrs. Stuart teaches it?" Esther asked.

"Yes. You're all invited. It's a great group of women. We don't just workout. We bond, we relate, and we get to spend quality time with Bridget and Paisley. I know Bridget would be happier with you girls in the group."

"Or some boys," Sophie said, elbowing Esther.

"Come one, come all." Madison flung her arms out wide.

"It sounds great," Miss Priest said. "I definitely need to leave the library once in a while and do a little bonding. I'm also a pretty good cook. I could share some of my favorite recipes and maybe get some new ones."

"It's a wellness journey. We are finding our authentic selves—peeling away the layers we hide in. Melissa is brilliant. She's training to be a life coach as well as our wellness coach. Please, you must join us at least once."

"What times do you work out?" Sophie asked.

"We work out Tuesday and Thursday at 4 p.m. at the brick church on the hill, and Saturday mornings we will work out in the new park, weather permitting, at seven thirty in the morning. Bridget can pick you up."

Esther stepped back. "We have to help Parker finish a project this week."

"I might try a Saturday." Ms. Priest smiled. "Is the park open?"

"Oh yes, but we haven't had the official ribbon cutting ceremony. We are saving that for the summer when tourists arrive. I'm just glad the city approved it. We've needed some kind of arts or a theatre in the area. We don't give our children enough culture and opportunities to explore their creativity. Having an amphitheater and concert stage will allow us to enrich the lives of everyone in Coho County—don't you think?

"Ms. Merriweather," Sophie said. She cocked her head and folded her arms. "I have a quick question. How is an outdoor amphitheater on the Oregon Coast going to work when we get on average over one hundred inches of rain on more than half the days in the year?"

"Sophie!" Esther put her hands over her eyes. She couldn't watch.

Madison laughed musically. "Oh, my dear, I do adore you. Not to fear! We have a large sloping glass roof over the round stage. And in the future, we will build a twin glass ceiling over the audience."

"Did you plan the event on social media? You know, the one called, *The End*?" Sophie studied her face. "If you did, it's genius. It made me curious."

"*The End*?" Madison's brows drew together, and she look up, thinking. "I wish I had. Fascinating name, *The End*. But not to worry. It's a public park. I am sure they have a permit or something."

Ms. Priest gently put a hand on Esther's and Sophie's shoulders "Well, I love the backdrop of the Stonehenge replica on the cliff with the ocean behind it. I hiked to the park last week. It's gorgeous. And the terraced seats are a feat of engineering that blends in with the landscape. I think we need to thank Ms. Merriweather."

Madison grinned broadly. Esther thought, if she didn't have so much makeup on, she might be blushing. She shook her head, and her earrings made a tinkling sound. "I did it entirely for me. Not only is it a tremendous write off, but I am also going to launch my newest book at the park. The unexpected bonus has been the amount of time I hope to spend with my Bridget and you amazing young ladies. Sophie, you're a caution."

Sophie brows gathered over confused eyes. "A caution?"

"Google it. Now girls, Ms. Merriweather and I have a short meeting." Ms. Priest shook her head and she and Madison exchanged knowing looks.

"Is it in the urban dictionary?" Sophie asked Esther.

Esther shook her head, no.

"Cynommon, why don't I treat you to a cup of coffee at the Coffee Shack. We can talk on the way?" Madison said.

"Can you girls take care of things if I'm back in ten minutes?"

"I'll keep Sophie under control Ms. Priest." Esther said. "Let's try looking up 'you're a caution' on the new tablet, Soph."

"I'm googling it now." Sophie was rapidly typing on her smartphone.

Chapter Three
Flash Mob

Esther turned on the gas log in the library's ancient stone fireplace. They settled on a rug on the floor in front of the flames, leaning back against a large black leather sofa. Esther added the college brochures and application instructions she'd printed out during her online search to Sophie's pile.

Used to working efficiently together, they quietly sorted the information by institution, distance, and quality of education. The Ivy Leagues were lined up closest to them.

"Because we're juniors, I feel like time is short. We only have one more year to make sure we have what it takes to qualify for schools or scholarships. Stanford and California aren't as far away as Yale or Georgetown. I mean, Oxford would be my first pick, but lately I've been thinking, I've never traveled anywhere outside of Oregon or Washington." Esther picked up an admissions form.

Sophie picked up another brochure. "You wouldn't be alone. I would be there, and I've traveled, sort of. I've visited Grandma in Hawaii, and gone with my parents to places like Las Vegas and Washington D.C."

"It's not really the travel. Well, it sort of is. It's more the Oceanside High Library, the ocean, and . . ." Esther bit her lip. "And I would miss Parker and Nephi, wouldn't you? Nephi hasn't decided where he wants to go."

Sophie looked up at Esther. "Nephi, huh? So, let me be sure I understand. What you're saying is, we need to find out where Parker is going and that will influence your decision." She wiggled her eyebrows at Esther and chuckled.

Esther shook her head and shrugged. "I don't know."

"I guess we better ask them," Sophie said. She picked up another college brochure and opened it.

"No! I know it's lame, but when I think about leaving this school and Necanicum, I get a little anxious. Don't you?" Esther said.

Without responding, Sophie put down the colorful booklet she was reading. "We're in trouble."

"Why? What does it say?"

"A suggested essay question in more than one of these applications is to reflect on your involvement in improving your community or school and why the project you chose was important to you." Sophie picked up another booklet and opened it. "This one asked for a list of your involvement in one or more activities as a volunteer in your community. The last one I looked at wanted one or more ways you contributed to your local school or community."

Esther closed her eyes. "Doesn't our work in the library count? I am sure Ms. Priest would write us a reference."

"Nope. We get graded for it, and we were paid for tutoring last summer. I haven't volunteered for a single thing except events Paisley organized with the boosters and our parents."

The library doors opened and the janitor, Simon, came in with a younger man in a red shirt. "Bob, you start upstairs. Make sure your measurements are exact. Include the locations of the outlets. You will be judged on neatness. Remember, you're the guy in the red shirt." Simon handed the man a pencil and slapped him on the back, chuckling. "Relax." Simon's brown eyes folded into his ancient wrinkles, and he let out a hearty belly laugh. He shook his head and rubbed his gray hair.

The young man climbed the short metal stairway to the mezzanine, and the rarely used Athol Peacock Meeting room, dusty encyclopedias, and a rare books section.

Esther realized Simon hadn't seen her or Sophie. She whispered to Sophie, "What is he doing?"

Simon turned toward the sound of her voice while adjusting his hearing aid, which let out a high-pitched squeal. He closed his eyes in frustration until it stopped. "Girls? What are you doing on the floor?"

"Doesn't the guy in the red shirt in Star Trek always die?' Sophie said.

Simon laughed loudly. "Yes, but don't tell Bob. Red shirts were always expendable on Star Trek. I love that show. What is all this?" He waved his hand over the college brochures. "And what are you doing?"

"Just making a college wish list and deciding which schools to apply to," Esther said.

"I see. But why on the floor?" Simon asked.

"We're by the fire because it's cold today. Why is he measuring the plugs? Are we finally getting a computer?" Sophie said.

"I already installed a notepad." Simon smiled. "Doesn't that make you happy?"

"Almost done, boss." Bob called down to Simon. He had a medium build, medium brown hair, and plain features. Vanilla, except for the bright red shirt.

Simon laughed his easy laugh again and looked down at the girls. "He's my new guy in training. He has to wear the red shirt until we're sure he's a keeper. We've hired him to help with tech and electronics."

"Oh, so he isn't a janitor?" Esther said.

Simon shook his head and put his muscular hands in the pockets of his brown jumpsuit with the Oceanside High wave and his name embroidered on the breast pocket. "We can't afford tech around here. Officially, in the school district budget, he's a 'ja-a-a-nitor.'" When he said the word janitor, he made air quotes. He looked up the stairs and called loudly, "And a junior janitor as long as he does a good job."

Sophie closed her brochure. "Are we getting more technology? Please, oh, please?"

The library doors opened again and a middle-aged man in an expensive golf polo and bright green and yellow plaid slacks entered the library without noticing the girls. Esther was surprised to see a very rare frown flicker on Simon's face. His entire countenance fell.

Esther had seen the man in the golf pants before. She knew he was the school board chairman, but she couldn't remember his name. He was holding rolled papers that she suspected were blueprints.

"I told you this place is awful, dark, dank. It all has to go." He waved an arm over his head and swung it around. "The entire thing is so outdated our students are suffering."

It was like a lightning bolt to Esther's heart. Without thinking, she jumped to her feet.

Startled, the man put his hand on his chest and took a step back. "Oh, young ladies. You surprised me." His firm face softened into a syrupy smile that stopped at his hazel eyes, which lay flat under his perfectly styled brown hair.

Sophie marched passed Esther and stood in front of him with her fisted hands on both hips. "What's wrong with the library? It's nothing a few computers couldn't cure."

He didn't even flinch. He held his hand out to Sophie, who didn't take it. "Lars London." He waited and then pulled his hand back. "That's exactly what I hope to do." He turned to Simon. Esther watched his sappy smile completely disappear. "Measure it. Our meeting is this afternoon. The whole thing needs to be scrapped for a bank of computers and a research library. What we really need is an entirely new building out of the tsunami zone. Not only is this one falling apart, but it is in a dangerous spot if we have an earthquake."

Ms. Priest came in the west doors with the ocean breeze. Madison, still smiling and laughing was right behind her.

"You're early." Madison beamed at Lars London like he was an old friend.

Again, Esther watched his face change into a condescending smile under the same flat, hazel eyes. "I have a little meeting with Principal Kelly. The International Timeshare I work for is going to make an important donation to the school" And with that he left the way he had come in.

"Hello, Simon." Ms. Priest smiled but her eyes narrowed, and her brows drew together. "What's going on?"

Simon's mouth opened, but no sound came out. This went on for a while before he said, "Ah. They asked us to measure and record the location of all your outlets. We are also to get the room measurements for the school board meeting."

Madison pulled her chin in, stood to her full height, and said, "I'm on the school board. What's this really about?"

"I have no idea," Simon said. "I just do what I am told." He stepped on the bottom stair and called, "Bob! Are you done yet?"

A wide-eyed Bob looked over the railing, nodded rapidly, and quickly took the stairs.

"We'll stop interrupting your day." Simon nodded. "Ladies." He was gone so fast the library doors swung back and forth for a moment until they came to rest.

Sophie broke the silence. "The chairman said he hates the library, and it all had to go."

Ms. Priest turned to Sophie. "What?"

Sophie nodded. Ms. Priest's mouth fell open and color rose in her ivory cheeks.

"He also said, the building is in a tsunami zone, and we need a new one," Esther said.

"I don't know what's going on, my dear, but I am going to get to the bottom of it." Madison strode out the double doors. "Lars, wait for me." Ms. Priest was right behind her. The doors swung back and forth in the heavy silence.

"Should we go save him?" Esther asked.

"Let her tear him apart," Sophie said.

Chapter Four

Closed Group

Esther looked up from the new tablet in the library. "Sophie, I just remembered we have counseling today. We can't go for lunch. I better text Parker. I hate missing him. I'm dying to know what his surprise is."

"I am too. Do we have to go to counseling? I think we're fine." Sophie sighed. "I know Mr. Mephisto is trying to help and all, but do you really think we need it?"

"Do we have a choice?" Esther loaded her backpack. "I mean, I know he volunteered to see a lot of students as the school counselor after the murder at the dance, but I think he focused on me because . . ."

"Your dad?"

Esther looked down at her feet. "Yes. At first, I went because mom told me she wanted me to see him about my bio-dad. Mephisto admitted she'd called him right after he arrived at Oceanside High. She probably called him at about the time my bio-dad walked away from the Prison Work Release program and tried to kidnap me."

Sophie's eyes opened wide, and she put her hands on her hips. "Your dad was messed up. If I was your mom and my ex tried to kidnap you, my daughter, and then started writing to you and wanting you to write back, the answer would be short and clear. N. O. No." Sophie wagged a finger like a scolding parent. "Didn't he end up working with sex traffickers? You don't need a therapist. You need an attorney who can keep your dad parked in solitary confinement. I mean, he tried to kill your mother, for cherry pie's sake."

"I used to agree, totally. But now . . . I didn't used to believe people could change as much as my dad would have to for me to trust anything he said. I'm glad all we've talked about during counseling so far has been the ball, and how traumatic it was to come so close to losing Parker. I don't want to think about the past with my bio-dad. I just want to be normal, you know? Not the girl who survived the infamous dad story."

"There is no normal. Normal is a myth. What I want is an abnormally huge cheeseburger. I know we've always gone to see Mr. Mephisto together, but seriously if your mom is serving spinach smoothies for dinner and I haven't had some cheese and grease, I'll die." Sophie buttoned up her sweater. "What if I don't go to Mephisto's counseling, just this once? I could go with Parker and bring lunch back to you. What do you think?"

Esther closed her eyes and rubbed her forehead. "I don't know. I mean, I feel bad. I want to do both."

"Parker will understand, I promise, and then we'll meet you back here for a quick bite in half an hour. Mephisto doesn't keep us for much past thirty minutes. Deal?"

"Deal. You know me. I just want to do the right thing. I would just be anxious if we stood the counselor up," Esther said.

Sophie smiled at her. "And you know me. Food is king. I know your favorite since grade school is chicken nuggies with four fry sauces and extra fry sauce, right?"

Esther smiled, pushed her glasses up on her nose, and nodded.

"I'll be back soon with food." Sophie ran for the west door where Parker's car would be filling up with Nephi, Paisley, and Bridget.

My heart says go with my friends. Someday, I need to unbutton the cardigan and surprise them all. Just play, Esther thought as she walked to the school counselor's office.

Students passed her happily heading for the lunchroom. Jackson, a friend and student from their class, gave her a quick hug.

"How's the artwork coming along?" Esther asked.

"Thanks for hooking me up with Madison. She got me into an art school and a mentor to work with me on art for her first illustrated book," Jackson said.

"Don't you love how generous she is?" Esther said.

He nodded. "I am totally grateful. Lunch calls." He waved and trotted down the hallway.

Nephi gave her a quick wave as he passed her on a run for the parking lot and lunch without her. Familiar faces of kids she'd known most of her life looked at her, nodded, or were so involved in conversation they didn't even notice her before she slipped into the guidance counselor's office.

Oceanside High School had a student body of around three-hundred students and two school counselors, Miss Wanda for the seniors and students who needed extra scholastic support, and Mr. Mephisto who saw all the other students. He had joined the staff shortly before a shocking murder that had occurred a few months ago during a school dance. She remembered seeing Mr. Mephisto at Simon's house planting flowers when he first came to town. He'd lived next door with Simon until he found a place of his own.

Mephisto had sprung into action immediately following the tragic incident at the ball. He'd organized trauma services for some of the other students who had witnessed the death of Aiden Van Doren, a booster club member. He'd arranged for affected students to meet with crisis counselors from the local mental health provider. She was surprised by the number of students who signed up for help.

In an odd way, she trusted him a little. She wasn't sure why, except that he treated her with a kind of respect no one ever had shown her before. He always reminded her that she should have more control in her life. He didn't treat her like she was broken.

Esther was far more impacted by Parker's brush with death and hospitalization than Van Doren's death at the time of the ball.

Esther remembered Parker's erratic behavior before he went by ambulance to the hospital during the dance. Parker and Van Doren had both been drugged by Van Doren's jealous girlfriend. Van Doren, a wealthy school booster had been declared dead by the time he got to the hospital. Parker was in intensive care for days.

The feeling of total fear and memories of her and Sophie's hunt for the drug that had poisoned him, still made her heart race. But Parker was fine, and so was she. She had survived worse with her own father before he went to prison.

Mephisto had taken Esther aside in the middle of the chaos and insisted she let him help her personally. She could still see it. He had taken off his gold, wire-rimmed glasses and looked at her intently with his watery, hazel eyes. He said he'd made special arrangements to meet with her at the school and handle her trauma recovery himself. He said it was important to start immediately.

She agreed, but only if Sophie could come with her. *No wonder Sophie's not interested. She has a happy family and bounces back the way I might if I had a normal family. She's not as big a mess as I am. Thank heavens I worked with him. He forced me to be better and do better when I'm triggered.*

The guidance office was as quiet as the halls were noisy. Esther sat down.

Edna, the secretary, was busy on her computer. She didn't look up. She chatted softly on a headset attached to the phone.

"Esther." Mephisto was standing in front of her.

She smiled and got up. She'd been so deep in thought she hadn't even heard him coming.

Mephisto's office didn't have any windows. He had one shelf with a variety of books, crystals, and plants. His desk was in the corner. A large red leather chair faced a bright yellow couch he offered to students. Between Mephisto and Esther was a retro avocado green sixties coffee table with a rectangular sand tray and toys on top. It had a tiny rake, seashells, a plastic dog, and an angry looking ceramic man that resembled Principal Kelly. Sophie was always playing with it.

"Where's Sophie today?"

"She had a conflict." Esther didn't offer anything else.

"Good. That will give us a short chance to talk about something that has been on my mind."

Esther studied his face. He put his manicured hands together in front of him, making a steeple with his fingers. He didn't say anything. He let the silence hang in the air. Esther didn't flinch.

A smile turned up one corner of Mephisto's mouth. He sat back and smoothed down the sides of his short brown hair. Esther realized that when he smiled, one long gray hair peeked out of his nose. She quickly looked down at the floor.

"Esther?"

She looked up, and their eyes met. He leaned forward, elbows on his knees, looking intently at her.

Ignore the nose hair . . . don't stare . . . don't stare . . .

"Your mother originally called me about your father. Also, some of the teachers told me he went to prison after trying to take you away from your mom. They also said you were badly bullied on social media following the kidnapping attempt."

She sat back and looked right at the nose hair, frowning. "I'm okay."

He raised his eyebrows and drilled into her skull, eye to eye, without looking away.

Before she knew what was happening, she felt angry, triggered, and for some odd reason started crying. She sat back, folded her arms, and took a deep breath.

He handed her a box of tissues. "Have you had any contact with your father?"

She didn't want to answer. *I should have gone to get burgers. I want Parker and Sophie. I want fry sauce. I hate thinking about this.*

"It's common for parents in prison to reach out to their children and ask for forgiveness, try to stay in touch, or ask you to do things for them. Have any of those things happened? Has he written to you?"

Her head snapped up at the word 'forgiveness.' *Why does everyone want me to forgive him? What if I'm not ready? Why am I here?*

"Have you had any contact with him, Esther?"

"You talked to my mother? I'm sure she told you that he sent me a letter."

"Actually, she didn't tell me he'd written. I used to work at a homeless shelter. Some of the men I counseled had been in prison. That's why I know it's normal for prisoners to write to or even try to manipulate their family and friends. What did his letter say?"

"He wants me to forgive him."

"Have you written back?"

Esther studied him. She wasn't sure she could trust anyone but Sophie and her family with the intimate details of her life. "Yes."

"Esther, I want you to know that you absolutely are not obligated to write him back or forgive him. And no matter what anyone says, you have every right to be angry about what happened. I've read the notes in your file. As a matter of fact, I would like to help you set boundaries and work on finding peace with this issue. You might find you're ready to leave this toxic relationship behind."

Esther sat up again and let out all the air she was holding while she waited for his opinion. *Well, this is new.*

"Would you let me help you?" He slid to the edge of his seat, still grasping both hands in front of him. *Does he ever blink?*

She thought for a minute. "You know that everyone else has been telling me to forgive him or to hate him forever. My pastor says to give it to God. What am I supposed to give God? What's your idea of help?"

"My idea is to listen to what you want and support you as you make that happen." He opened a wooden box, which sat next to the tiny sand tray. Inside were flat, round rocks. He took out one that fit neatly in the palm of his unusually small hand. "I want to help you release the weight of your past traumas. When you're ready to heal, you will be able to identify things like your father, memories of trauma, or even friends you need to let go of to move forward. My hope is we can write what you choose to give up on these stones. Then, when you're ready, we will release it all into the sea and let it sink all the way to the bottom. I can free you of the weight you carry." He set the stone down in the sand between them.

Chapter Five

Influencers

Esther left the counseling office so preoccupied that she didn't see Simon and Lars London until she rounded the corner and ran into Simon's back.

Embarrassed, she tried to go around him. "Sorry." Lars London was facing Simon. Both men stood silently until she was further down the hallway. She kept her head down, wishing she were invisible.

After she rounded the corner, she couldn't help it. She had to know what was going on. Hiding behind the wall, she looked back at the men and listened.

"I am not selling my house at any price to you or anyone else," Simon said.

"We've made you a more than fair offer," London said.

"I understand what you're up to. I've seen your little meetings with Principal Kelly." Simon's voice got louder. "There are some things in this world that are more important than your money. This school is part of this town's history and so is my home. No one is going to tear it down for any reason."

Simon was leaning over London and pointing his finger at London's chest. Every part of London, from his frown, his fisted hands, and his boxer's stance looked angry. As if they felt her eyes, they both looked down the hall.

"We'll talk again." London's arms dropped to his side, and he turned his back on Simon and headed her way.

"Not if I can help it." Simon's large ring of keys jingled as he walked the other way.

Esther quickly slipped inside the library doors and watched London leave the building.

⌒

"Less than an hour to go," Sophie said.

"Not soon enough today." Esther put a stack of books on the cart. Principal Kelly was in Ms. Priest's office, leaning over the desk, annoying her with his usual dad jokes.

"Why do seagulls fly over the ocean?" Principal Kelly said. Before Ms. Priest could answer, he began laughing at his own joke. "Because if they flew over the bay, they would be bagels?" He laughed hysterically.

Simon and Bob were moving tables and chairs for the school board meeting.

"Principal Kelly," Simon called. "What did the janitor say when he jumped out of the closet?"

"I don't know, Boss," Bob said. "What did the janitor say when he jumped out of the closet?"

"Good job buttering up the boss, Bob," Sophie said.

Simon chuckled and finished the joke. "Supplies! Get it, Supplies, like surprise?"

Bob's face looked blank. Esther waited. Bob blinked and then his face lit up and he laughed.

"You've got to be quicker to impress an old man like me, Bob. Now take that end of the table. We're moving it in front of the fireplace."

The couches were pushed aside. Bob and Simon set up a table with chairs for the school board members.

After Simon left, Esther and Sophie finished the set up with rows of chairs facing the table. Esther put a clipboard on the library desk with a sign-in sheet and then stood back to check their work. Sophie put a cup of pens by the sign-in sheet. ⋅

"I've counted the pens. I am putting out ten," Sophie said.

"Ice-cream bet on how many are left after the meeting? I say three." Esther grinned.

Madison came through the west doors with a large bag and an impressive looking briefcase. She was back to looking like herself with a stylish black dress and heels.

"Esther, Sophie?" Ms. Priest said. "You girls can go upstairs and study in the conference room until the meeting is over or run home and come back to help clean up afterwards."

"We'll stay." Esther nodded, gathered her things, and followed Sophie to the mezzanine.

Sophie put a finger to her lips and pulled her toward the conference room and shut the door. "Let's lie down by the chairs near the rail and watch the meeting. I'm dying to know what his plans are for the library."

"Good idea," Esther said. "Maybe we should record it."

"Why not? I'll get as much as I can with my phone or until the battery dies. We can post it on social media and get other kids to help us make sure Lars London doesn't do anything to our library."

Esther nodded. "Let's spread our stuff out on the floor near the rail in case anyone comes up to check on us. We want to look productive."

They went to the rail overlooking the meeting. Principal Kelly was nowhere to be seen. Ms. Priest and Madison were talking at the desk.

"I want you to meet Simon," Ms. Priest said. Madison followed her to where the two men were working. "Simon, this is Madison Merriweather, the author."

They were talking so quietly, Esther only caught every other word like garden, house, and then something about a job. Simon nodded a lot. After a few minutes, Madison gave him one of her famous hugs and left Simon behind, smiling.

Gradually, the school board began assembling along with spectators scattered in the audience. Principal Kelly moved until he was seated by Ms. Priest, who quickly got up and excused herself, moving across the aisle to sit alone.

"I can't believe Principal Kelly is still chasing around Ms. Priest," Esther said. "Didn't the school board give him a warning?"

"That's what I heard. He doesn't seem to care," Sophie said.

Lars London banged a gavel on the oak table.

"Where did he get that?" Sophie whispered. She and Esther were lying on their stomachs between two leather chairs peering over the edge. Sophie had her smart phone propped up on a book, so that it captured the meeting.

Esther shook her head. "I bet he carries that gavel around for fun."

"We'll call this meeting to order. I'm Lars Joseph London, board chair. Will the other members introduce themselves?"

"This is going to take forever," Esther said. "Don't chew your nails."

Sophie stopped chewing and looked at her, rolling her eyes. "I'm bored already."

Madison introduced herself.

The woman to Lar's right gave him a knowing smile. "Candy Sharp, vice chairwoman. Thank you, Lars for doing such a great job at leadership." She clapped lightly. No one joined her, except for two older women further down the table.

"Gillian Johnson." A woman next to Candy stood. They had matching short and spikey haircuts. She looked at Candy and giggled before she sat down.

"I'm Merry Spencer, owner of the wine tasting shop."

"Jennifer Schmidt, Oceanside High student parent and newest member. Thank you for coming." Jennifer wore workout clothes with an Oceanside High Soccer Mom tee shirt.

An older woman in a gray polyester jacket stood up. "I'm Louisa Johansson and this is my best friend from Oceanside High Class of '62, Betty Karlsson, and our friend Jack Abner, class of '60 or Oceanside High's last state-championship football team." She gave herself a rousing hand of applause and Jack and Betty stood up beside her, smiling.

Jack wore a school sweater. "Go, Gray Whales!" He made a spouting motion with his hands over his head.

Sophie slapped her forehead and it echoed. Luckily, everyone was looking at Jack Abner.

After basic business was out of the way, Madison was next on the agenda.

"As you know, I plan to be a long-time resident of Coho County and now, Necanicum City. I've purchased a little house near the new park and am excited to offer to the school use of the new city amphitheater for school productions. Sadly, however, I've learned that the arts were cut from the budget several years ago to make way for more STEM classes and improved state test scores."

She took a sip of water from a glass on the table and stood. "As someone who makes a living using her creativity, I was alarmed when I heard that the arts weren't deemed a priority. It's one of the reasons I ran for the school board. I've spoken to Principal Kelly and would like to offer use of my musical consultant to the school. I hired him to produce the music for the movie based on my book. He is willing to be available to the school at my expense." She motioned for someone in the small audience to stand.

A medium-sized man with a brown ponytail and wire-rimmed glasses stood up. He wore corduroy pants and a worn-looking sweater with leather elbow patches.

"Doctor J. Willard Phelps has graciously offered to provide one music class a day and lead any artistic endeavors the students participate in as far as drama, the stage, or concerts. He is a graduate of Julliard, and taught at several prestigious institutions in Maine, Virginia, and most recently Seattle, before each school cut their arts programs. I hired him as my daughter Bridget's piano and voice instructor and the musical consultant for my films. He is a multi-talented educator who starred in and directed off-Broadway plays. He has a double masters in the arts, education, and his doctorate as a licensed music therapist."

"What a resume," Sophie whispered. "And he's cute."

Esther nudged Sophie and crossed her eyes. "No way . . . cute?"

Sophie giggled softly. "Who's sitting next to him?"

"No clue," Esther said.

Doctor Phelps sat down. Esther hadn't noticed the boy next to Doctor Phelps until Sophie pointed him out. He had black hair, cut short on the sides and wavy on top. He sat forward with his elbows on his knees, pulling his white t-shirt tight across his muscular back.

"Doctor Phelps and I, with the help of my daughter, have a written a one-act play." Madison said. "All the board needs to do is to approve the project, and to provide insurance for practices and the event. I'll match that with a donation of a year and a half's salary for Doctor Phelps. I will also provide him with additional money for basic housing while he teaches at the school, and basic classroom supplies."

The audience burst into wild applause. Lars London banged the gavel multiple times before Madison sat down, and the room quieted.

"Madison, it is not necessary for you to tell this town what to do and how to raise their kids," Lars London said. "If my kids want music lessons, I supply them, as I am sure all the other parents do. The arts aren't going to employ these kids. They need to accept that they live in a rural community, and we need to support more education around local trades."

A man in the audience shot to his feet. Esther recognized him. He was a world-famous artist that lived one town over.

Lars London banged his gavel loudly again. "We are not taking audience comments at this time."

The man was red in the face, so red that the color was moving over his bald head. He remained standing.

"Sit down." Lars banged the gavel again, and the man finally sat slowly.

Louisa Johansson jumped to her feet and was followed by her best friend, Betty. "Bravo, Bravo! Madison, we graciously accept your extremely generous offer."

Lars banged the gavel so hard, Esther waited for its top to pop off. "Sit down!" While the room quieted, London leaned forward and massaged his temples. He looked up and around the room. "What do we do next, Jack?"

Jack Abner opened a book and sat silently reading for a moment. "According to our bylaws and policies, we can take public comment or just vote. We have to have a majority before a decision can be made. Anything involving funding over a certain sum, requires a district-wide vote. This doesn't sound like it will cost enough to require that."

Lars sighed heavily and looked sideways at Candy, who reached over and patted his arm, then rubbed it for a minute. He patted her hand.

"Gross. Did you see that?" Sophie said.

"I think I threw up a little," Esther said.

Turning his attention back to the room, Lars London said, "Alright. We'll take public comment for a short period of time. But if it gets out of hand, we are going to cut it off and vote. Is that allowed, Jack?"

Jack adjusted his glasses and consulted the book again. The clock ticked. He nodded at Lars.

Lars said loudly, "Note the record." Candy takes notes. "Those wishing to comment can line up behind the microphone. Please speak up for Louisa and Betty." The best friends snickered.

Esther watched the artist go first. He was well respected in their town.

"I have made a wonderful living for my family with my art. My brother, who also grew up here, has a band that has played around the world and sustains his family. I sell paintings in the United States and Europe, that I paint right here in your town. My wife writes novels. They may not sell as well as Madison's, but they pay the bills. We have to stop saying the arts aren't an important part of our society. Maya Angelou's poems changed the world. Charles Dickens's books educated leadership. Songs written by my brother's band raised money to feed the hungry in Africa. I will add a personal sum to Madison's donation." The room burst into applause as he held his hat in his hands and looked down, blushing while he walked back to his seat.

The next speaker was the mother of one of the girls in Esther's summer tutoring group. She was a bright girl but struggled with math.

The lean woman spoke softly. Lars banged the gavel. "Speak up!"

She shook visibly. "I am a parent of a student who is a gifted singer. She sings all day long at home. There isn't a song she doesn't know. I have always wanted to get her music lessons, Mr. London, but I don't have your privileges. I clean hotel rooms in the hotel my husband manages. We have four children, including one with cancer. It would be a dream come true for my Trudy to be able to take music at school. I believe she has a gift and could contribute great things in the world."

"Every parent thinks their child is gifted," Candy said to the room. A rumble ran through the crowd.

Madison stood. "I say let's put it to a vote."

Betty jumped up, "I second that."

Lars shook his head. He was clearly outnumbered. "All in favor, say, aye."

Everyone but Lars, Candy Sharp, and Gillian Johnson voted in favor.

Jack read the numbers and said, "The motion passes."

Suddenly Lars perked up. "The next motion on the agenda is a request to provide the students with a research library and a facility so students can earn CTE credits, or the Career and Technology Education required for today's higher education opportunities and jobs. Why, one class could teach a student how to register guests at a hotel or operate a computer for sales in a retail job. They could learn to install cable."

Many parents in the room applauded.

Madison stood up. "Mr. London, where do you suggest we build this classroom or research library?"

"Right here." He waved his arms around, indicating the library. "This library is outdated. We need to install floor to ceiling windows and better lighting, multiple outlets, and a computer on every table. We don't need a rare book section or conference room, we need laptops and Zoom."

"I object, your honor." Jenifer jumped to her feet, surprising Esther. "I mean, I have something to say. For the record, I limit my kids screen time. They already know how to lead virtual meetings and know more about technology than anyone at this table. Tech has been a part of their lives from the time they could walk. I don't understand why we have to lose one thing to add another?"

Candy jumped up. "Well, where else do you suggest we put it? Huh?" She looked at Lars and laughed.

"I have an idea," Lars said. The room quieted. "If we don't put it here, we rarely use the auditorium. Why don't we remove the auditorium, put in the research lab, and put a portable stage in the lunchroom?"

Ms. Priest jumped to her feet and approached the microphone in front of the table.

"We're done taking comments, Ms. Priest," Lars said, and banged the gavel three more times until the room quieted.

Ms. Priest was shaking. Esther had never seen her like this. Her hands were fisted, and her face was fire red. "You don't have to take my comment, but it will be said. That auditorium is as old as this library. All the town meetings in the late 1800s were held in the auditorium. During the Tsunami of 1964 half the town slept in that room. The carvings, the velvet drapes, the handmade features, including the original theatre chairs, make it priceless and not something to be tossed aside for something a student carries in their back pocket or that is taught in a classroom. Computers become obsolete. Books never do. Have you opened one up and smelled it? Books are magic." Half the room jumped to their feet and applauded.

Simon approached the mic. "Mr. London. I'll go to the auditorium tomorrow and do a safety check. I don't see any reason why the auditorium should be deemed outdated or dangerous. There is also a music classroom with an entrance backstage and outside on the north end of the west parking lot."

Madison clapped, and the rest of the room joined her.

Lars banged his gavel again and again. "A tsunami is exactly why we need to consider student safety. Look outside the west doors to the library. What do you see? I'll tell you what you see—the river in the estuary and a few hundred feet away you see the mouth of the river and beyond that the ocean! Scientifically, Oregon is overdue for a large earthquake, which would trigger a tsunami. There is nothing between the water and these kids in a tsunami."

The room was silent.

Simon stood up, head down, humble. "I don't know about tsunamis. That's another discussion entirely. But I do know about safety and this building. I will begin checking the building for safety at the auditorium tomorrow morning.

The crowd clapped in agreement and smiled at Simon, nodding and giving him a thumbs up. Esther knew tsunamis were always on the horizon, the stuff nightmares were made of. But this school was one of a kind. More than half the people in the room had students at Oceanside high and had experienced dozens of tsunami warnings. They were a hearty people.

Esther watched Lars scan the room. Then he scowled at the clock. He was clearly outnumbered. "Look at the time. I move we set this aside and discuss the research library offline before returning it to the board for a vote." He banged the gavel, stood up, and quickly marched out the door without looking back.

Esther watched people chat and mill around the room. Sophie took random photos. Eventually, Esther was bored and began texting Parker. She opened the online invitation to *The End*. Whoever was hosting it had added more photos. There was a black and white of her favorite mini mart across the street, a photo of a seagull on a school bus, and a photo of Simon on his porch earlier in the morning.

She scrolled through the event invitation, noticing students posting photos of themselves with the hashtag, "*The End.*" She Googled #theend. It brought up random pictures, including a few well-known serial killers, people with faces painted like skulls, drawings of coffins, and other random things like a headstone surrounded by daisies. "Gross. Look at this Sophie." She showed her what the hashtag brought up. Then she pulled up the event and scrolled past local students' photos of themselves at the park or just doing something silly. Their pictures were hashtagged, *The End*.

Sophie shrugged. "Geeks and weirdos, gotta love them. Selfies aren't for me." She held her phone up, leaned into Esther, who smiled, and took a selfie.

Esther looked back at the photos and kept scrolling. The last photo was a picture of Ms. Priest, talking to Simon on his front porch. He looked concerned. Ms. Priest's back was to the camera. Anyone walking to school or in the drop-off lane could have taken the picture, but for some reason, it sent a shiver up her spine and made the small hairs on her neck stand on end.

Chapter Six

Post-Worthy Foodie Fun

"Charcuterie board!" Esther's mother, Grace, made a rare appearance in the double garage at the back of the James' house. She was dressed in workout clothes and had her curly, blonde hair up in a ponytail and carried a bread board with apple slices, cheeses, and rolled meat slices. Mary stood next to her holding a jar of peanut butter and a plastic knife, looking like Esther's mom's mini twin, except for Mary's heart-shaped sunglasses, and layers of bling around her neck, wrists, and fingers.

Esther cringed and looked at Sophie who was helping her sand Parker's 1964 classic seventeen window VW van. Bridget poked her head out of the driver's side window and gave them a knowing look, wagging her eyebrows.

"Nephi, will you go up and bring down the bottled water?" Grace smiled and set the tray of apples down on the long workbench near the wood-burning stove.

"It's okay. We have soda pop in the fridge." Nephi pointed at the battered garage fridge in the corner decorated by greasy handprints and surf stickers.

"Is it diet?" Grace walked to the fridge.

Nephi leapt up, beat her to the door and leaned on it, folding his arms and grinning sheepishly.

"Nephi . . ."

"We'll eat the meat and cheese. Promise. We love apples."

Grace laughed and looked at Papa J. "Don't let them totally sugar up, okay? It's time this family took better care of our health."

Papa J's head bobbed up from the engine compartment. "Nephi, go get the water."

"I'll help you," Parker's twin sister, Paisley, said.

Nephi's arms dropped, and he rolled his eyes at Papa J, but he followed Grace and Mary out of the garage and around the house to get the bottled water.

"It's okay guys. Grandma Mable drove us to get donuts after school." Sophie pulled a box out of the cabinet under the tool bench. "I have chips, popcorn, and candy. I think we're safe."

"Bring me one." Papa J grinned like a naughty child.

"She is going to kill you," Esther said. "Shouldn't you be setting a good example?"

"Party pooper," Papa J said from behind the van.

Parker leaned around the end of the van, chuckled, and winked at Esther. She gave him a mom-face, shook her head, and kept sanding the primer with fine-grit sandpaper and water.

"How much longer do we have to keep sanding?" Sophie asked.

"Long enough for my surprise to show up." Parker went to the fridge and opened two diet pops, bringing one to Esther and kissing her on the cheek.

"Turn the other cheek," Parker said. She laughed, and he kissed her other cheek and handed her a greasy pop can.

"Thanks?" Esther looked down, half smiling, with a single dimple. She glanced at his happy face while she vigorously cleaned the can in the sink. "Parker? You know how much we love the library and Ms. Priest?"

"More than you love me?" He gave her a cheesy grin.

"Get over yourself!" Sophie yelled from the front of the van.

"Well, let me think . . . the library or Parker?" Esther tried to frown and look at the ceiling.

Parker pulled a maple bar out of the box. "Can the library give you a maple bar?" He waved it in front of her. Esther wiped her hands off and reached out to catch it. "Uh, uh! Me or the library? Let me show you how handsome I am." He struck a pose, winked, and wiggled his eyebrows up and down at her.

"Alright!" Esther snatched the maple bar. "The library. It has books! You know they're my first love." They laughed together, but Esther quickly stopped. "Actually, Ms. Priest and the library have been my sanctuary. When life stinks, the library remains the same."

"Things change," Sophie said. "Like the new tablet for checking out books. It isn't all bad."

She watched Parker's face for any sign of recognition.

Parker chewed on his lip and looked her in the eyes. "I get it. When we lived on the estate in England, my grandfather's desk was in the library. No matter what was happening, he would let me come in, find a book, and hang out with him."

She smiled. "Exactly."

"When mum started asking my father to move closer to her parents and the states, the library was the thing I thought I would miss most, besides our dogs and the horses. But as it turns out, it's my grandfather I really miss."

"Is he a caution?" Sophie asked.

Parker threw his head back and laughed. "Definitely."

"Now, I'm being serious. Bridget, help me," Esther said. "Bridget's mom may be the only thing between Lars London, the school board chair, and our library. And if he can't have the library, he'll go after the auditorium."

Sophie put down her sandpaper, stretched, and stood by Esther. "He wants to bring in more computers and technology, which is good, but he proposed putting them in place of the library."

Esther nodded. "You should have seen Ms. Priest. She was fierce. She gave him a history lesson, and he ended the conversation fast."

"Yeah, but not before Simon agreed to look at the auditorium," Sophie said.

"Who is this guy? Lars London?" Parker asked.

"He is the school board chair. He had Simon measure the library," Esther said. "I don't think Simon wants anything to do with changing the library. He loves the school and is going to retire soon."

Parker rubbed the back of his neck, leaving a grease smudge under his blond hair. "What about you, Papa J? You're a police officer. Don't you guys know everyone?"

Papa J wiped the grease off his hands with a red rag and took a powder-covered donut hole out of the box and popped it in his mouth. He chewed for a minute. "I think I do." White powder puffed and covered his lips and part of his navy-blue t-shirt. He began brushing it off and brushing grease on his shirt with the rag while he continued. "He's the guy who built the monstrosity a little further south on the beach. You know that huge timeshare with the awesome pool and hot tub you can see from the sand, but you have no hope of using unless you own a time share? Anyway, I guess he and some others own it together. That's why he ran for the school board."

"I don't get it?" Parker said. "What does one have to do with the other?"

"During his campaign he kept talking about the need for top-notch education, so local businesses could recruit quality staff. He promised to create jobs for local high school graduates. He said improving local education would prevent crime by connecting kids to job training."

Bridget hung out the side window of the van. "That's just money talk for I want the community to approve my project and not tax me to death."

Papa J laughed, loud and hard. "When did you get so smart, Bridget?"

"Listening to my mother," Bridget said from inside the van. "Mom won't let it happen. She'll just buy the building."

Parker laughed loudly before going back to work on the engine. Esther took her hair out of its ponytail and habitually pulled it all back into a messy bun. One curl refused to comply and fell over her left eye.

"Boys." Sophie exhaled and rolled her eyes. "Esther, you and I, ice cream at midnight. We are going to figure out how to keep the library. It's like telling Batman you're making his cave into condos or selling the Watch Tower for a timeshare.

Esther couldn't help it—she grinned. "Or like tearing down Hogwarts to build a parking lot."

"Right on, Sister."

Bridget leaned out of the van window again. "Hey Parker, did you see the event online? You know, *The End*?"

Parker laughed. "Are you kidding me? I don't have time to go online. You're sailing through school while I'm buried in AP Chemistry. All I do is work on the van, school, and what my parents tell me to do. Why? Do we all want to go?"

"Maybe. Here, let me show you." Esther pulled her cell out and searched for the event.

When she looked it up, Nephi came back, carrying a case of water. Paisley held one bottle, which she had opened and was sipping. He dropped the case inside the fridge and took out a bottled root beer.

"Here," Esther said. She handed her phone to Parker.

"Isn't that Madison's park? What did they name it?" Parker said.

Esther looked over his shoulder. "The Stone Circle."

"It's cool. The replica of Stonehenge looks real. I remember going to Stonehenge with our grandfather."

"The host and people are posting random pictures of the town or saying they're going. Look." Esther pointed at a photo of Ms. Priest and Simon talking on the steps of his house next to the school.

"Yes, but what do you . . ." Parker stopped talking. He frowned and turned the phone towards Esther.

A photo was added to the event, just below the picture of the park. It was of Esther and Sophie going into Oceanside High's front door with Bridget.

Esther shrugged. "There are a lot of kids besides us in that photo."

"Yes, but I don't like the idea of someone photographing you without asking, much less using it for an advertisement." Parker narrowed his eyes and zoomed in on the photo. "It makes it appear that you're planning on attending or are hosting the event."

"I haven't figured out who's hosting it." Sophie joined them, looking at the photo.

"Bridget," Esther said. "Is this your mom's event? Is that why she wanted to park this morning at drop off? To get a picture of us?"

Bridget called from inside the van. "Let me see." She leaned out the window and Parker walked the photo over to her. "Great. They got a photo of my backside. I'll never wear those jeans again."

"I brought you . . ." Grace stood in the open garage doorway holding a tray of cut watermelon and strawberries. Her mouth was hanging open.

"Sorry, honey." Another puff of powder came out of Papa J's mouth as he hid a white donut hole behind his back.

She raised one eyebrow. "I see how it is. Just remember, sneakiness never was happiness. Mary will want one." She took a maple bar out of the box and left after taking a large bite.

"Do you think she'll tell my mother I'm eating junk?" Bridget said.

"You're doomed," Sophie said.

"Are you really writing a play? Is the play for her book launch?" Esther asked.

"Yes." Bridget climbed out of the driver's side of the van. "Will you come to the play?"

Esther paused her sanding and listened to the distinct sound of tires on the gravel.

"My surprise!" Parker shouted. He bolted for the open door. His father parked a small truck and got out with his mother.

"What is it?" Esther was right behind him, trying to see in the back of the truck.

"Wheels and tires!" He was grinning from ear to ear. He hugged her and picked her up off her feet before he dropped her and climbed into the truck bed. "I feel a road trip coming on! Nephi, give me a hand."

Papa J looked in the truck bed and whistled loud and long. "Nice!"

Chapter Seven

BRB

Ms. Priest wasn't in the library when they arrived. Esther turned on the lights in the main room. The first bell rang and the noise outside the library picked up, as did the sound of lockers banging shut. She took the key out of the coffee cup on the desk and unlocked the drawer holding the rubber stamp.

"Do you think I should try turning on the new tablet?"

"Not without training." Sophie chuckled and hung up the white hoodie she had borrowed from Esther.

"Do you want to get out the college applications again and work on them?" Sophie asked.

"It feels fruitless. Maybe we should first come up with a community project or a way to volunteer that we can put on our applications. What do you think?"

"You're right. It's not like we can buy a park, like Bridget's mom. We could volunteer with Mr. Stuart at his clinic, but I am not big on barf, blood, and guts."

"Me either," Esther said.

Sophie held up her hand. "Wait . . . wait . . . I know what we can do! Why didn't I think of this last night? It's great for the community, the school, and it's easy. We can get help and we don't have to pay for it or raise money for the project."

"It sounds too good to be true," Esther said.

"It is!" Sophie held a personal small celebration. She put her hands up and danced while saying, "Yes! Yes! Yes!"

Esther crossed her arms and raised one eyebrow. "What?"

"It's genius. We offer to lead, plan, and help Madison produce her one act play and musical that Bridget is working on. We invite Paisley and Bridget to help us. Paisley won't be able to stop herself. She'll take everything over. Bridget's mom will want her daughter's experience to be a success after I explain how important the project is for Bridget's college application—and we will be able to check the box while being sponsored by Madison. We'll have a team that can't be beat! And! The best part? We get to put, 'Assisted world-famous author, Madison Merriweather, to bring the arts to a small rural community,' on our college applications." She threw both hands up in the air and ran like a crazy person, in place. "Yes! Yes! Yes!"

Esther high fived Sophie and did the yes dance with her for a full minute. The library door opened and the boy who sat by Doctor Phelps at the board meeting came in. Both girls were breathing hard. Esther couldn't help it, she giggled. He didn't say a word. His dark brown eyes got larger, and he just backed out of the room, all six-foot three inches of wide eyed, raised eyebrow and shock.

The door shut, and both girls laughed uncontrollably. They were still gasping for air when Esther said, "I love it! Do you think Madison will let us help?"

"I don't know why not?" Sophie said. She wiped tears from the corner of her eyes. "Since we're going to be using the auditorium and music room for our project, let's go take pictures and check it out. It will give us an excuse to wander the halls all the way to the vending machines and stock up on celebration candy."

Esther relocked the stamp drawer and turned off the main light. "We should look at the class behind the stage. We might as well, in case she lets us help for our community project." She peeked out the door. Bob, still in his red shirt, pushed a mop bucket toward them with a squeaky wheel. "Janitor Bob is out there."

"Relax, E. Just walk confidently. Look like we're supposed to be in the halls, you know, official." Sophie pushed the door open and, with her head up, marched out of the library. "Hi Bob." She nodded without smiling at him. He stopped pushing the bucket and watched them walk in the opposite direction down the empty hall.

When they passed the open cafeteria door, they walked faster. The smell of spaghetti and sour milk wafted out of the vacant lunchroom. Esther could hear pots and pans, running water, and the cooks talking over the noise. Someone laughed loudly.

They turned toward a little booth in the wall. The Boosters used the booth to sell hotdogs and drinks at basketball games. The vending machines were at the end of the dark hallway, by the doors to the gym. The lights in the vending machines shone like an oasis in the windowless hallway.

"I only have a dollar fifty. What do you have?" Esther fished in her jeans pocket for more money.

Sophie held up a small coin purse. "Mom left me a hundred dollars in small bills and change so I could pay my own way if your family went anywhere. We're loaded."

Esther's eyes lit up, and she snickered quietly.

Sophie put in a five-dollar bill in the vending machine and read numbers to Esther, who gathered the change when it fell.

"It's so noisy."

Sophie looked over her shoulder. "I don't hear anyone coming. D-6."

Esther fed the coins back into the machine and Red-Hot Bites fell into the tray. Sophie fished them out.

When they both had three packages, Esther buttoned her cardigan. "Here, give me your candy." She tucked the bottom of her sweater in her jeans and filled it with the candy. "I have a nice little candy baby." They laughed.

Esther quietly patted her belly. "Shush. We're going to get caught." The giggling only got worse.

Sophie motioned toward the auditorium, on the west side of the building, directly across from the gymnasium. "Let's go."

They noiselessly crossed the hallway. Esther tried the doors. "Locked. I know another way. I used it when I left the last assembly early."

Esther led Sophie back across the hall, into the dark gymnasium, and down into the girl's locker room. "There's a door in the back, so if you're acting on stage, you can use the locker room as a dressing room and bathroom."

"I didn't know that. I guess I've seen the door, but never bothered to open it."

Esther pushed the door. It didn't open. She stepped back.

"Try harder." Sophie gave it a hard push with her shoulder and the door opened, making a grinding sound, and groaned as the rusty hinges worked. Stale, dusty air blew in their faces.

Esther's heart jumped, and she looked around to make sure no one else heard the noise. The hallway behind the door was pitch black. She pulled her cell out of her pocket and used it as a flashlight.

Sophie held onto the back of her sweater. "E, how long is this hallway?"

Esther could hear her blood rushing in her ears. "It wasn't this dark when I used it before. Plus, there was a lot of us. It goes down to the basement level and back up behind the stage. It's genius really. I guess there is another tunnel that leads to the boy's locker room."

"It's a good thing I don't believe in ghosts. I'm surprised more students aren't sneaking down here." Sophie chuckled, and it echoed.

The ground beneath their feet began to level off.

"For what?" Esther said.

Sophie laughed harder. "What do you think?"

"To get out of class?"

Sophie snorted. "Right. To get out of class."

The ground began to rise. "We're almost there."

"You're such a good girl, E." Sophie let go of her sweater and they stood side by side at a metal door.

The light on the other side of the door seeped into the hall from underneath the door, but the heavy darkness they were immersed in still made Esther's heart race. "What if it's locked?"

"I don't care. I'm getting out of here." Sophie pushed the metal bar on the rusty door and Esther with it. They stumbled out backstage. "Where are we?"

"It's the furthest corner of backstage. I've been back here before." Piles of dusty furniture that were probably used as props were stacked against the brick wall. Above them, ropes draped down from the ceiling in semi-organized chaos. There was a ladder running up the back of a wooden cutout in the shape of a tower with wheels. She looked up. "This place is so cool. Look at the catwalk." They wandered through the obstacle course. "Listen. Did you hear something?" She put her arm out so Sophie would stop walking.

"No. Simon must have left the stage lights on. He said he'd be here during the meeting," Sophie said.

"Was that the sound of a door closing?" Esther asked. They waited. Nothing.

"Keep going," Sophie said.

Esther led the way to the back of heavy red velvet curtains.

"Is this the stage?"

"No," Esther said. "These are the curtains that keep you from seeing behind the stage. We're still backstage." She pushed the curtains, looking for an opening. The thirty-foot-high curtains released dust and parted a few feet away. "I wonder how wide the stage is? These curtains are massive."

Sophie sneezed. "I'm allergic to dust." She sneezed again.

"You sound like your shiatzu, Spam." Esther pulled the curtains apart for Sophie to go through and screamed. Grabbing Sophie's arm, she pulled her back behind the curtain and held it shut, gasping for air. She looked at Sophie and realized her ears were ringing from Sophie's scream. She had to look again. It couldn't be real. Sophie's nails dug into her arm while she slowly opened the curtains again.

Center stage, framed by a red spotlight, lay Simon. He was face down, with his head at an odd angle and an arm clearly broken. Sophie spun her around, her mouth open, eyes wide behind her round glasses, and then they both turned back to the gruesome scene. "I . . . I . . ." Sophie let out another short but piercing scream.

Blood rushed in Esther's ears like a fierce waterfall. She couldn't think. She ran to Simon's side and watched to see if he was breathing as she felt for his pulse. Nothing. Kneeling beside him, she put her hand over her mouth. Bile rose. She held her stomach, trying not to throw up. Next to her, Sophie stood frozen, bathed in red light.

A tall extension ladder cast its shadow across his back and the stage. A large yellow measuring tape was still clipped to his hip.

"Sophie, he's not breathing. He's dead."

"Are you sure?"

"Shouldn't I . . ." Esther touched his neck again. "I'm not a nurse. I can't find a pulse."

"He must have fallen off the ladder," Sophie said.

Esther put her hand over her pounding heart. Looking around the seventy-foot-wide stage, she took a deep breath and let it out slowly. "There. Did you hear that?"

Sophie's head snapped up, and she spun around, looking in all directions. "I heard it this time."

"It's underneath the stage." Esther looked around the stage for a trap door or a way down to the orchestra pit. The podium the principal used during assemblies was lying on its side with broken glass around it. The microphone was almost twenty feet away, still attached to the cord, but in pieces. The chairs that sat behind the podium were turned over and scattered. Photos printed on plain paper were spread around like garbage underneath Simon and in bits and pieces everywhere. "Soph? Do you see what I see? I don't think he fell off the ladder. Wouldn't falling knock the ladder over?"

Esther heard a sharp intake of breath. Sophie was bending over the body, reaching towards it.

"Don't touch anything! We need to call 911. Remember Ashley? We almost got put in jail for tampering with the evidence."

"Look." Sophie pointed down at his back. His arm was pulled in close to his chest, and there was something in his hand. "It's like he was trying to protect it. We have to know what's on that paper."

"Shouldn't we just call 911?"

"And have Kohornen show up, decide it's an accident, and go home for a nap before school is over?" Sophie said.

"You're right . . . Wait!" Esther took a picture of the body with her cell. "Before we do anything, take a video of the entire stage and email it to me. Let me get the paper in his hand so we can look at it." She pulled her sweater sleeve over her hands, steadied herself, and got in closer. She pulled his hand out, being careful to keep the sweater between her and the body.

"What is it?" Sophie asked.

"I don't know. It's blank, I think. She got in closer and tipped her head. "Wait. There's something on the other side."

Esther reached out and pulled the small, folded piece of paper from his hand. She awkwardly tried to unfold it with her sweater covered fingers. It finally opened. It was a picture of her. She dropped it. Her hands flew over her mouth, she heard herself gasp, and she squeezed her eyes shut and opened them. It was still there. Laying on the floor. Time slowed down while she reviewed her life searching for the moment captured in the image. Why would Simon have her school picture?

"Shut the front door!" Sophie snapped a photo.

"How . . .?" Esther asked. Her voice shook. "I don't understand."

Sophie reached out and finished opening the folded photo.

Esther looked over her shoulder. "That's my school photo from last year. Someone's written my first name on it. I don't recognize the handwriting. We shouldn't have touched it."

Sophie turned it again and refolded it. She held it out for Esther. On the back of the paper in light pencil the words, "*The End*," were hastily scribbled. A shiver ran up Esther's spine.

A door closed somewhere in the theatre, echoing. Her heart jumped. Footsteps ran from the lobby door towards them in the dark.

"Girls!" Mr. Mephisto ran up the stairs on the far side of the stage and headed toward them. He dropped to his knees and felt for Simon's pulse on his neck, like the girls had. Then he picked up a photo, mouth open, and took out his phone. "Hello? Police? There's been an accident. We need an ambulance. No, I can't find a pulse . . . What's the address? The auditorium at Oceanside High. Why the address? The high school!" He shook his head in disbelief and said to Esther, "I know this is traumatic, but you girls need to get out of here, now."

"But . . ." Esther said.

"Go!" Mephisto barked in Esther's face. Pointing towards the lobby doors. He frowned. His face was sweaty and red. Squeezing his eyes shut, he ran his hands through his normally perfect hair, leaving it sticking up like a mad man's. "You shouldn't be here! Go straight to my office and let Edna know the police are on the way."

Esther backed away. *I still have the picture of me in my hands.* Sophie gave her a knowing look and kept typing on her cell phone.

"What are you doing?" Mephisto asked Sophie.

"Trying to call my mom." Sophie made a ridiculous frown and sniffed loudly, turning her back to him.

"Go!" He growled.

Still typing, she and Esther walked past the stairs to the balcony. They both walked slowly to the hall doors.

"Wait," Sophie said. "Over here." She pulled Esther behind a large column between the two sets of double doors leading from the auditorium. She went back to typing.

"What are you doing?" Esther whispered.

The main door opened, and Bob the janitor ran past them without seeing them. He sprinted down the aisle to the stage. Then a screamer entered the dim light.

Madison Merriweather had both hands over her mouth and eyes opened wide, still screaming, she staggered past them without noticing them. The new chorister, Doctor Phelps, was on her heels, pale, looking all around as if danger was lurking everywhere, except behind his back where the girls hid.

Bob took the stairs to the stage two at a time and fell to the floor on the other side of Simon. He shook Simon's body.

Madison didn't get very far before she squeezed her eyes shut and collapsed in a seat. Phelps grabbed her hand and began patting it rapidly. He looked at the stage, at Madison, and then back to the stage. He let go of her hand and backed up, tripping over his own feet while running for the exit.

The girls stepped deeper into the darkness behind the plant.

"Soph. We've got to go to Mephisto's office. He said to!" Esther hissed.

"Give me a second. I'm just emailing myself the photos and video I took in high resolution so I can delete them off my phone. It will take a minute with the schools Wi-Fi. I have to delete them before . . ."

Sirens interrupted Sophie. The girls looked at each other and left the shadows for the closest door. Esther pushed it open slowly and peeked out. Officer Ironpot's large frame was running on his massive legs towards them.

Esther shut the door. "Ironpot. He'll call Mom if he sees us. She'll freak out." They stepped back behind the palm tree.

Ironpot barreled through the doors. "Back away! Don't touch anything! Is he alive?"

More sirens. Different sounding sirens. The doors blew open again and Principal Kelly ran into Ironpot's beefy arm as he clotheslined the principal, stopping him dead in his tracks.

"Everyone! Off the stage! Now!" Ironpot said.

Esther took advantage of Ironpot's fury as a cover for their quick exit. When she got to the door, she slowly pushed the metal bar, hoping it didn't squeak as it opened. Then she and Sophie slipped through.

Ms. Priest stood across the hall, eyes wide with concern. Her mouth fell open and melted into a scowl. She pointed at the library and the girls walked silently back to their sanctuary with a furious librarian on their heels and the candy still in Esther's sweater.

Ms. Priest opened the door to her office and turned the lights on. With her eyes narrowed, she pointed at the chairs facing her desk. The girls walked in silently and sat in the wingback chairs. She closed the glass door behind them.

"What just happened?" Ms. Priest asked. "Why are the police here and why were you sneaking out of the auditorium? You were supposed to be here, watching the library."

"We just . . ."

"It's not our fault . . ."

Both girls starting talking at once and stopped in unison. Ms. Priest looked at both of their solemn faces. Esther's chin was pulled in and she stared, blinking rapidly. Sophie pushed her glasses up and kicked Esther's chair.

"You tell her." Sophie looked at Esther, leaned back and swung her short legs back and forth, calmly.

Esther head snapped around and she gave Sophie a quick, cross-eyed look and shook her head, no. Sophie just winked, while Esther gripped the arm of her chair so hard, her knuckles were white.

Taking a deep breath, Esther started telling Ms. Priest their bright idea. "You see, Soph and I found out we have to do a community project if we ever want to get into a college that is on our list of preferred schools. We realized we've never done any community service without being paid, which doesn't count as volunteering. Even when we weren't paid, someone else, like Paisley organized it. Well . . . "

Ms. Priest closed her eyes and rubbed her forehead. "Just skip to the part where you decided to leave the library unattended."

"Soph had this great idea."

"It's a great one, you should hear it." Sophie leaned forward.

Ms. Priest held one hand up in Sophie's direction to quiet her. "Continue please."

"We were just taking a quick trip to the vending machines for celebration candy, because the idea was so good. Then we were going to the auditorium to gather information for the idea. But when we arrived the doors to the auditorium were locked. So, I showed Sophie how to get in through the girls' locker room."

"What?"

"Yeah. There is a great passage between the stage and the gym. I bet there are a dozen passageways in this old building."

"Esther." Ms. Priest raised one eyebrow and shook her head.

"Oh yeah. Back to the story. So, we got to the stage. I thought I heard someone there, so we might have heard the killer."

"Killer?" Ms. Priest leaned forward, and her angry face softened into a look of concern.

"Simon is dead," Sophie said.

Ms. Priests hands flew to her mouth, and she ran for the door. Before the door could close, Esther's mother, Grace, and her sister Mary came into the library.

"Essy!" Mary called.

Her mother burst into the office, "Esther!"

Esther jumped up and threw up in the garbage can. After the dry heaves ended, she sat back with her hands over her sweaty face, crying for Simon. Packages of candy fell from her sweater to the floor.

The office door opened and the tall boy from the meeting smiled, realized Esther was losing her lunch, and then he quickly retreated. He put his hand over his own mouth and ran for the door.

"We are not going to leave a garbage bag of barf in Ms. Priests office," Esther's mother said.

Ms. Priest hadn't returned and with all the police presence, medics, and the chaos of parents arriving to pick up their kids early, her mother insisted Esther leave with her.

Carrying the bag of barf, with the top tied in a knot, ahead of her like nuclear waste, her mother parted the chaos and led Sophie and Esther to the parking lot. Sophie held Mary's hand so she wouldn't fall behind and get lost in the crowd. Her mother dropped the smelly bag in the cement garbage can outside the school.

"Who told you to come?" Esther asked. "I mean, I'm happy you're here but how did you know?"

"It's Coho County," her mother said. "Everyone has a scanner, and our closed online group and group text notify us when a bear sneezes in the woods or where the roadkill is on the highway. Papa J texted me. He thought you would be upset about Simon. He was a really sweet old guy."

"Where were you?"

"Mary and I were at the store buying bottled water for the work-out class this afternoon. Do you two want to go? I can't leave you home alone at a time like this. Death is never easy, especially when it's unexpected."

"Do they know who did it?" Esther asked while she climbed into the front seat of her mom's SUV.

"Who did it? I heard it was an accident. No one did it. It isn't anyone's fault."

"Who told you that?" Sophie leaned closer from the back seat.

"It's what the group said, online. They're usually right."

Esther fell back in her seat, closed her eyes and rubbed them. "It's not an accident."

"Esther James." Her mother backed up and got in a long line of cars. "Not everything is a murder. Accidents happen." She handed Esther a pack of gum from the ashtray.

"Well, this didn't happen accidentally. I know it." Esther's stomach rolled again, and she rolled down the car window, hanging her head out in the fresh air.

"Esther, what did you do?" her mother said.

"Nothing. I swear it."

Mary kicked her seat. "You're in trouble young lady."

"Mom!" Esther said.

"No, she isn't. Don't kick the seats. Apologize to my car, Mary." Her mother rolled through the last stop sign before their house. "You do smell a bit, Esther. We need to talk after you clean up."

Esther made it in the door and fell face down on the couch.

Sophie sat in the nearby chair. "I'll explain it to her."

Her mother sat on the coffee table facing Esther. "Okay, tell me what happened."

"Do you want me to tell her?" Sophie asked. Sophie knelt on the ground next to Esther's still form on the couch.

"It doesn't matter," Esther said into a pillow.

Her mother patted Esther's back. "Yes, it does. Death matters. Especially when it is a nice person like Simon. Kohornen will get to the bottom of it. The online scanner group, you, and I can speculate. He can't. Let me get you a cold washcloth, something to drink, and crackers. You're shaking."

"Sorry I barfed." Esther pushed herself up and looked at Sophie.

"No worries. Some days are very stressful." Sophie got up and fed her fish, The Angel of Death. "I'm already problem solving. Some people throw up when they are stressed, some people clean, or eat a whole tub of ice-cream. You and I are going to figure out what happened to Simon."

Mary crossed the living room. "You got mail." She handed Esther a letter addressed from the *Point of The Mountain Correctional Facility*.

Esther laughed softly and then a little hysterically.

"Chocolate?" Her mother sat in front of her with a bowl of ice cream, Selzer water, and saltine crackers. "Chocolate is good for the soul on hard days."

Esther grimaced. Her stomach rolled violently. "No thanks, Mom." She closed her eyes and drifted off to sleep and dreamed. Flashes of memory wandered in, out, and around like pieces of a puzzle.

Chapter Eight

News Feed

Esther washed her face with a cold washcloth. "I need to change my clothes. I stink."

"Seriously. Okay. I joined the scanner group." Sophie scrolled on her phone.

Esther crossed the hall. Without looking up, Sophie followed her to her room and sat on the bed. "Here it is."

"Already?" Esther tossed her clothes into her laundry hamper and dug out her favorite torn jeans and softest hoodie.

"It's a small town, girl." Sophie shook her head. "Harvey Bart says police have determined it was an accident. Prayers for the victim, Simon."

"Harvey Bart is a pretty dependable guy. He owns the new little cab company. I bet his drivers hear it all. Isn't his son-in-law an officer?"

"In Cabbott's Cove. Here's an article by Roger Abbott on the Necanicum News's social media page. 'Accident at Oceanside High.' He says the victim won't be named until their family is contacted."

"Why do they assume it is an accident? Will there even be an autopsy?" Esther stepped into her flip flips.

"Kohornen gets to decide. I don't understand our local detective at all. It's like the police always jump to the easiest conclusion." Sophie kept scrolling.

"I hope Papa J can help us. Do you think he'll be upset that we took pictures of Simon and the stage?" Esther said.

"Probably. He's protective of you. I can hear him, now." Sophie pulled her chin in, flexed the muscles in her skinny arms, and spoke in a deep voice. "You girls need to leave the investigating to the police. Oh sure, Kohornen couldn't find his reflection in a mirror, but you're just going to have to trust him."

The girls laughed so hard, Esther snorted. "Hey, now. He is the expert. What if he's right, and it's just an accident?"

Silent for a moment, their eyes met. "Nah," they both said. The giggling started again.

"Stop! Be serious," Esther said. "Can you still smell the barf?" She spritzed herself with perfume her mother gave her last Christmas.

"Uh, huh. The perfume gives the barf a floral scent. But the smell of throw up is coming from your laundry basket."

"Great. I have a garbage bag in the bathroom. I'll seal it in." She retrieved the bag, filled it, and tied it shut. Esther pulled her hair up into a messy bun on top of her head. "We haven't heard from Nephi or Parker. I'm going to text Parker and see if they're together."

Sophie stood up. "Wait. Hold on. Hold. Look at what someone posted on *The End*." She held out her phone so Esther could see the screen.

Esther's heart dropped. Her stomach lurched again. "That's . . . that's where we found Ashley's body on the beach. I don't understand. Who put that up?"

Sophie looked at the new photo. "The caption just reads, 'Remember the good times.'"

"That isn't funny. It feels threatening," Esther said.

Sophie nodded. "I've been wondering. Do you think Mephisto told them we were there? No one has called to talk to us yet. You would think they would by now."

"I don't know. Maybe he's trying to protect us. What do you think?"

"He works for the school. Eventually he'll tell our parents or the principal. Either way, we need to talk to your parental units first and give them the details."

"I guess. Every time I close my eyes, I see Simon's body. He was so nice. I can't imagine the school without him. No matter what Kohornen believes, I think in Simon's honor, the truth needs to come out." Esther heard a car door close outside. She went to the window. "Parker and Nephi are here. So is Papa J. He's early and still in uniform. I thought he was working until eleven tonight."

"Let's go see if he has heard anything he can tell us," Sophie said.

"Okay. What really gave me the creeps were the photos. Whatever happens, Simon knew about *The End*, and somehow the event and his death might be connected. The photo of the spot Ashley died feels like it's pointed at us, like a set up. Like whoever is posting photos is playing with us."

"Do you think they're pointed at us, or everyone?" Sophie asked.

"Right now? After that picture? At us. Maybe . . . I don't know. Let's go downstairs and see what Papa J knows."

After Esther quickly brushed her teeth, they went to the stairs. Esther stopped at the top of the long circular staircase and turned to face Sophie. "Do you think we should tell Papa J we took a photo out of Simon's hand and kept it?"

"I'm not sure. What do you think?"

"I don't know either. Should we wait?" Esther took a deep breath and blew it out slowly. "Maybe. Let's just see what he has to say."

Esther started down the two flights of stairs. "Well, here goes nothing."

⌒‿

"Esther! Parker's here." Nephi called up the stairs.

"Why don't you just text like normal people?" Sophie rounded the last flight of stairs before Esther.

"Is she coming down?" Nephi asked.

"I'm right here." Esther said.

Parker met her on the bottom step. "Are you okay?"

The tears started again. "Don't ask me that question. It makes me cry."

Parker hugged her until she was breathing slowly.

"I'm fine." Esther gave him an unconvincing smile.

"Right . . ." Nephi rolled his eyes and folded his arms.

Parker looked down at her until she looked back at him. "I've never seen you like this."

"Seriously. I'm fine." Her voice raised. She stepped back and out of his arms. "Soph and I just need to talk to Papa J."

"I'm here." Papa J stood by the fireplace, quietly waiting.

"Esther, you need to rest. Here, have a soda." Her mother held out a can of lemon infused water.

"Ewe," Sophie said.

Esther couldn't help it. A giggle bubbled up and escaped. She could feel everyone in the room relax.

Nephi picked up the can. "These are gross. It's like a lemon burped for the flavor before they sealed the can."

Esther put her hand over her mouth, but another giggle escaped. "We should tell you all something." A giggle punctuated her statement.

Sophie's eye grew to match her round glasses. She raised her eyebrows. "Are you alright?"

"No. Not at all." Esther took a deep breath and tried to blow it out slowly. "I'm sorry. That wasn't funny. I don't know what's wrong with me."

"You're finally losing it," Nephi said. "Dibs on your room when they haul you off in a straightjacket."

"Nephi!" Mable said.

"It's okay. It's been a long day. Too much sugar." Esther kept taking deep breaths until her breathing slowed down.

"Sit down Esther," Papa J said. She sat on the couch with Parker and Sophie. Papa J waited silently, giving her the same emotionless face Grandma Mable would give her until she spilled whatever was on her mind.

"Sophie and I found Simon. On the stage. Dead. He was dead."

After a sharp intake of air, Papa J's jaw flexed. His eyebrows drew together, and he leaned forward, making the leather in his duty belt squeak. "Go on."

Sophie elbowed her gently. "Do you want me to tell it?"

"Sure." Esther fell back on the sofa and folded her arms in an effort to control her shaking hands.

"Esther and I had this great idea about how to . . ."

Esther nudged Sophie back.

Sophie deflated. "Well anyway. We can talk about that later. So . . . Esther and I wanted to celebrate with a little candy. So, we snuck out of the library and . . . "

"Esther!" Her mother said in her mom voice. Papa J held his hand up but didn't say anything. Her mom frowned and slowly sat down.

"Sorry, Mom," Esther said.

Papa J nodded at Sophie. "Go on."

"Wow. You're a great cop. That was really . . ." Sophie said.

Papa J's head dropped, and he took off his hat and rubbed his forehead. "Sophie."

"Okay, Okay. So, we went to the vending machines. Oh, yeah. I forgot. We also wanted to get pictures of the auditorium for our—you're seriously going to love this idea."

Papa J cocked his head and raised his eyebrows.

"I know. Later. So, after we got the candy, we wanted to go to the auditorium to take pictures and check out the classroom behind the stage. So, we tried the doors in the hallway, but they were locked."

Esther nodded.

Sophie spoke with her hands. "Esther knew about the tunnel that goes from the girl's bathroom in the gym to behind the stage. You know, for the actors? Well, anyway. We took the tunnel. It was so creepy. Seriously creepy!" Sophie looked around to see if they believed her.

Nephi rolled his eyes and sat down on the fireplace hearth but didn't say anything.

"Anyway. When we were going to the stage behind the curtain, Esther heard something."

"No, I think that was later," Esther said.

"Okay. Well, when we got to the stage, the ladder was up, and Simon was on the ground on his stomach, but he didn't look right. The stage was a mess, like there was a struggle, and there were pictures in black and white. They were printed on regular paper, spread around him. And he held a folded paper in his hand." Sophie looked around the room.

"Go on," Papa J said.

Esther put a hand on Sophie's arm. "It was of me. It was my school picture. It had my name on it."

"But on the back, it said, *The End*!" Sophie said.

Parker's head snapped around and Nephi stood up.

Papa J pulled his chin in and rubbed it. "*The End*?"

Sophie nodded vigorously.

Papa J said. "I thought you girls learned with Ashley. How did you know what was on the folded paper?" His eyes bored into Esther's while one eyebrow slowly raised.

"Esther." Her mom's tone had changed from concern to the familiar firmness that came before a tongue lashing.

"I know!" Esther looked back and forth between them.

"I told you it was hard to have two parents when they both get mad at you," Sophie said.

"Sophie," Esther's mom said.

"Okay, Okay." Sophie sat back. Clearly done.

Papa J looked down at his hat in his hands, silent for a moment. When he looked up, he took a deep breath and blew it out slowly. "Well, at least Simon's death was an accident. I went to the scene right after the call. He didn't have anything in his hand and there wasn't any paper on the stage. It would have been impossible for anyone there to clean anything up that fast. As for the chairs you said were overturned. I didn't see anything disturbed but the ladder. It was leaning against the piano, so he could have fallen, and it could have hit the piano. You have got to stop tampering with things. If it was something other than an accident, you two could have been pulled into trouble again."

"You don't believe us . . ." Esther was shocked. "I've never lied to you." She reached back and felt the folded paper in her back pocket but didn't pull it out to show it to him. *Showing him the paper now would be like throwing gasoline on a fire.*

"I know, but it was a stressful moment. People often make mistakes when things like this happen."

"But I saw the same things." Sophie looked up at him, frowning. "It's the truth."

"This time, I actually agree with Kohornen. And besides, what is the motive? Being too nice?"

Esther stood. "We didn't do anything. But Papa, Kohornen is wrong. And . . ."

Papa J held one hand up, silencing her. "I hear what you're saying, and I understand why you'd feel that way. I've got to get back to work now. Please, don't talk to anyone about this for now." He looked at Grace and she nodded her approval. "When I get off, we'll talk some more."

Mary jumped up. "Is it time for class? I have to get my workout gear on."

Papa J smiled broadly, "Yes, goober, it is."

"I'll follow you out." Her mom followed him out the door.

After the screen door slammed, and Mary ran up the stairs to her room, Esther looked at Parker. "You believe us, don't you?"

"Of course, but it was awful. You know, stressful. It's easy to get overwhelmed. Like, what about all the photos? Where did they go?"

"I have pictures," Sophie said.

Esther took his hand. "I'm telling you. I promise. This wasn't an accident."

"Honestly," Sophie said. "If it was an accident, a ladder that tall would have fallen all the way over with him. It looked staged."

Nephi smiled revealing dimples. "It was a stage."

"Har, Har." Sophie pushed her glasses up her nose, rolled her eyes, and made a goofy face at Nephi.

"Let's go to the garage." Esther got up. "We can talk, while we work on the van."

"I'll get snacks." Sophie said. "Wait for me before you start."

Esther made herself a bottle of water and walked around the house to the garage. She found Parker opening the wood-burning stove. He sat looking at it for a minute. Then he put kindling it.

"The newspaper first." Esther held out an old newspaper.

He bit his lip and looked at her, taking the newspaper tentatively.

She couldn't help it. Esther broke into a broad grin. "Have you ever lit a fire before?"

"Sure. Loads of times."

"Can I help you?"

"I've got this." Parker pulled the kindling out and put a square of paper in.

"Crumple it." She chuckled. "The newspaper. You know, like this." She demonstrated.

He deflated and laughed with her. "I'm not great at this. We turn our fireplace on with a button. At my grandfather's manor in Britain, our housekeeper laid the fire."

"I finally found a chink in Prince Charming's armor. Here, let me show you." Esther took out the kindling and put the crumpled paper in the black stove. Then, she stacked the kindling and wood, expertly lighting the fire with a single match. She brushed her hands off and smiled at Parker, whose eyes twinkled, while he high-fived her. "Snacks!" Sophie came in the back door with a box full of potato chips, toaster tarts, a box of donuts, and a bag of candy. "I had to go to my house and raid the pantry. I needed to feed my dog anyway. You're never going to guess who is next door with the neighbor." She looked around the room, expectantly. "Okay. Guess."

"Who, Squirt?" Nephi said.

"Doctor Phelps. The music guy Madison brought in and the boy that was with him."

Esther shrugged. "So? The neighbor is a counselor. Maybe Mr. Phelps's kid needs therapy?"

"Who?" Sophie asked.

"The cute one that came in the library and sat with Doctor Phelps during the school board meeting," Esther said.

"Cute?" Parker said, studying her face.

She rolled her eyes and smiled. "Cute, like a puppy."

"You mean the tall kid? Yes. He was there." Sophie unpacked the food and laid it out on the tool bench. "He's cute, I guess. More handsome if you ask me. Did you show them the photo from the stage, or the picture of the place Ashley died?"

"Not yet." Esther pulled the folded paper out of her pocket. "But here is the photo of me that he had in his hands."

Parker took it and turned it over. "You naughty girls. You did steal evidence. *The End* . . . Isn't this your school photo?" He looked at Esther who nodded. He pointed at the words on the back of the page. "And that's the event, right?"

"See? It feels like a threat."

"Didn't you say there were a lot of photos? Couldn't they get them from a yearbook? Did they all have *The End* written on the back?" Parker asked.

Esther bit her lip. *He doesn't understand.* "Honestly. It feels like a threat," she said, again.

Parker studied the paper and turned it over a few more times. "I don't know. Maybe it was just the last piece in his hand. Was there anything written on the other pieces of paper?"

Esther closed her eyes and tried to remember. "Honestly? I don't remember. Do you, Sophie?"

Sophie shook her head. "I didn't see anything on the other photos, but that doesn't mean it wasn't there. Here, let me show you what's online, on *The End*'s page." She shrugged and pulled out her cell phone.

Esther watched and listened to Sophie catch everyone up. "After all of that happened, this picture showed up on that online event, *The End*." Sophie opened the event and began scrolling through new photos students had uploaded. Lots of chatter about Simon was uploaded with selfies. Finally, she found the photo of the beach where Ashley had died. She showed it to Nephi and Parker.

Parker looked over her shoulder. "Maybe they didn't mean anything. Maybe someone that knew Ashley and where she died posted it? Maybe Simon's death reminded them of the murder on the beach?"

"I'm with Parker. What happened to those little powdered donuts?" Nephi opened a cupboard.

Esther started scrolling. There was a new post. She clapped her hand over her mouth to muffle her response to what she was seeing. She looked at her friends, eyes wide, and turned her phone for everyone to see.

The new post was of Simon's hand holding the folded photo of Esther, pieces of paper blurry in the background.

"Who would take this? He's dead," Sophie said.

"We know he's dead," Nephi said.

"Yes, but he's dead in the picture." Sophie held up the phone for Nephi to see it.

"I know but . . ."

"In this picture!" Esther pointed at Sophie's phone.

She saw a look of understanding slowly settle on Nephi and Parker's face.

Parker took the phone and zoomed in on the photo. "Anyone could have taken this of anybody's hand."

"But that had to be taken before I took the paper from Simon's hand. See?" Esther held up the folded paper and her phone, side-by-side. "And it looks like it was posted by the event host."

Sophie leaned in to look closer at her phone. "But someone could fake . . ."

While Esther held out her phone, a new post popped up and the old one disappeared. It was a solitary photo of the ladder. Then one more photo loaded. It was the back of Sophie and Esther parting the curtains behind the stage. Sophie gasped. A surge of anger rose from deep inside Esther and burned through her chest, and across her face like red fire. Teeth clenched, she said, "Now do you believe us?"

No one said a word.

Waving her phone in front of their faces, she said, "Even if Sophie and I have to do this alone, we are going to find out what happened to Simon. Because someone was watching us, and someone is threatening us."

"Speak it, sister. We only saw Mephisto before Madison and everyone else arrived. Whoever was there and hiding could be the murderer." Sophie folded her arms and stood side-by-side with Esther.

"Mephisto?" Parker asked. "Where did you see Mephisto? Did he take this picture of you? This picture looks like a threat to me. Someone saw you were there, and they're sending you a clear message. The picture disappeared."

Another post loaded. It was a photo of little Mary in her workout clothes leaving the house with her mother following her. It had one caption. "And so it begins."

Chapter Nine

Bots

Sophie lived in a one-story beach house with a sunlight basement. The modern structure had a panoramic view of the ocean from every room except the state-of-the-art lab where her parents worked on their creations. No one really knew what they invented, but the lab was Sophie's playground as soon as she was potty trained at eighteen months old. Her old highchair with a five-point harness and tiny safety goggles still sat in the furthest corner by the eyewash station.

Nephi honked and Sophie came out of her house after she activated the security system. A security camera followed her down the walk. Sophie's mother's voice said, "Have a good day at school! We miss you!"

"Bye, Mom!"

Nephi put a piece of gum in his mouth. "I thought your parents were out of town."

"They are. Nanny cams." Sophie pointed at the camera by the grey wooden whale mounted on the stone near the entrance to the house. She opened the truck door and put her backpack on the floor.

"Did you feed Spam?" Esther asked.

"With a silver spoon." Sophie climbed into the truck, pushing Esther to the middle of the shared seat. Out of habit, Esther pulled the seatbelt around them both as they drove past Esther's house. Nephi rolled down his window.

"Phew," Sophie said. I am overwhelmed by your man perfume. She rolled her own window down and hung her head out.

"That's Maximum Override, my body spray." The truck bumped along the gravel road for the half-mile to school.

"Did you tell your mom about Mephisto and the online photos?" Sophie said.

Esther shook her head and held onto the dash. "No. She and Mary were gone already on an early morning walk with Parker's mom's group. Grandma Mable said Papa J was still at work. There was a big car accident that kept him past the end of his shift. Maybe we should find the workout group?"

"Nah. It can wait until after school," Nephi said and slowly rolled into the carpool lane. "Paisley told me her mom is working on a name for her program. I told her to call them Sweaty Moms."

"The Hot Flashes," Sophie said.

Esther giggled. "Beach Babes? Sea Skippers?"

"Curvy Coasties," Nephi said. Sophie snorted.

"Ripped Tides?" Esther flexed.

"Beached Whales." Nephi laughed. Esther playfully pushed him. He pulled past the circle in front of the high school and peeled off into the west parking lot.

"See you." Esther waved at Nephi. She and Sophie walked to the library doors.

Ms. Priest met them at the door and held it open. "How are you feeling today, Esther? I am so sorry about Simon."

Mr. Mephisto stepped out of the shadows as the doors closed. "Hello, Esther, Sophie."

Ms. Priest reached out and patted Esther's arm. "I hope you don't mind. After your reaction to Simon's accident, Principal Kelly thought you might like to meet with the counselor this morning."

Esther realized Principal Kelly was standing a few feet behind Mephisto.

Sophie's head dropped as she sighed heavily and let her backpack fall to the floor.

"We're doing okay," Esther said.

"I bought you some powdered donuts," Mr. Mephisto said.

"I guess we can meet for a few minutes," Sophie said.

Mr. Mephisto unlocked his office, walked to his desk and smiled as he showed the girls a box of powdered donuts from the local bakery. He took one out and put it on a napkin for himself and offered the box to the girls.

"Freshly baked donuts made by Jax. You know the new student— Mr. Phelps's son? He's working at the Sweet Stop Bakery. Fresh and homemade makes all the difference. Nothing better!" Mr. Mephisto took a bite of his donut.

Esther's mouth fell open when she realized that white powder had fallen down his usual sweater and was smudged on the very tip of his nose. She looked down, up, and then at the Sophie who had her hand over her mouth, stifling a laugh.

Sophie held her breath and then quickly grabbed a donut and stuck a bite in her mouth, chewing vigorously. She held the box out to Esther, who took it and put it on the table without eating.

"I still don't have an appetite," Esther said.

Mr. Mephisto leaned forward, and Esther had to look at the floor. "Oh Esther, your feelings are valid. Of course, you were so flooded by emotions that you threw them up yesterday and released your horror symbolically. Who wouldn't?"

"How did you know I threw up?"

"Bob the Janitor saw your mom carrying out the garbage and Ms. Priest guessed by the after odor in her office. She's gravely concerned about you." Then he sat back and looked at both of them, his donut paused in mid-air. "About both of you, of course."

Sophie brushed powder off her face and then began trying to get it off her black cardigan. She pushed her glasses up and looking at her hands tried to wipe them on her skirt. She took her glasses off to clean them.

"I am glad we get to chat," Mr. Mephisto said. "I was going to talk to you girls today, anyway. I hope you understand why Ms. Priest and I didn't tell the authorities you found the body. We discussed it, and she said they often jump to conclusions. We both just want to protect you." He raised one perfectly groomed eyebrow and looked from girl to girl. "So, we don't have to tell anyone unless you want us to."

"We talked to Esther's family last night," Sophie said. She leaned forward and studied his face fearlessly. "Is that a problem?"

"No. Well, um, I didn't say you were there, but . . . as an adult, I can be responsible for the consequences." He chewed on his lip, and Esther felt sorry for him.

"We don't want to get you into trouble," Esther said and offered the donuts back to him. He gave the box to Sophie.

Mr. Mephisto whipped his mouth. "I really wanted to talk to you about helping me plan a memorial service for Simon. I think it would be very therapeutic."

They sat silently for a moment. The only sound was the click of Sophie opening her phone to use it as a mirror and wipe the powder off her face.

"We just care about you girls."

Esther didn't know what to think. She looked directly at his powdered nose and then realized sweat was washing away the sugar.

Sophie stood up, and the donut box fell to the floor. She ran to the nearest garbage can and threw up. All the color drained out of Mr. Mephisto's face. He jumped up and put his hand over his mouth. "I don't feel so good."

"I never do when I see someone throw up," Esther offered.

Sophie hurled again. She turned to look at Esther. Sweat was running down her colorless face as she clutched her stomach.

"Help," was all she said. She dry heaved until Esther was sure she would turn inside out. After falling to her knees, she laid down, eyes closed, unresponsive.

Mr. Mephisto fell to his knees and threw up in the same can.

Esther opened the door to the office. "Help! Call for help."

The secretary looked past Esther to Mr. Mephisto hanging over the garbage can. She picked up the phone and Esther heard her say, "We need an ambulance at Oceanside High's counselor's office, as fast as you can get here. I suspect we might have a serious case of food poisoning."

Chapter Ten

Community Engagement

Esther ended her call. "My mom will meet us at the emergency room. She is on her way. She sounds freaked. She's calling your mom."

"No! I'm fine." Sophie tried to sit up, and a large medic named Edna pushed her back down.

"No, you don't." Edna started an IV as the ambulance jostled down the road.

Within only a few minutes of the secretary's call, the ambulance pulled into the hospital which was only two miles away from the high school. The driver opened the doors and Sophie's gurney was yanked out of the back, the wheels popped up, and they rolled it in with Esther following.

"I'm fine," Sophie said.

"You are as white as a sheet." Esther felt Sophie's clammy forehead.

"I'm fine." Sophie was awake. Her face looked green and grey.

Mephisto sat on his gurney with a plastic tub for throw up.

"Can it, kid," Edna said, and pushed her through the automatic doors while she shouted information at the nurses.

"What was she eating?" a nurse asked Edna.

"Donuts." Edna helped the nurse move Sophie from the gurney to the bed.

"I'm fine," Sophie said again.

"Did you bring the donuts?" the nurse asked, while she took Sophie's pulse, temperature and hooked her up to the monitors.

"No. They were in the throw up in the garbage can."

"Oh. Did they look funny or smell rancid?"

"No," Esther said, but no one heard her.

"What is that?" Sophie said.

"Charcoal." They crowded around Sophie and began feeding her black charcoal and working frantically on her.

"I'm fine!"

"Ladies! You can't go back there!" another nurse said.

"Yes, I can!"

Esther heard her mother's voice and peeked out of the small room they were in. "Mom?"

Her mother, Mrs. Stuart, Madison, and Mary came barreling down the hall in their exercise gear, only to be clotheslined by a formidable nurse. "Stop! Only immediate family."

"We are her immediate family," Madison bellowed.

"Who is her mother?" the nurse asked.

Esther's mom raised her hand. "I have power of attorney."

The nurse put her free hand over her face, closed her eyes, and shook her head. "Do you have it with you?"

"Yes." Esther's mom held up a piece of wrinkled paper.

"The rest of you, wait in the waiting room. You! Follow me. You too, short stuff." The nurse pointed at Mary, who adjusted her sunglasses.

Esther's mom gathered her up in a hug and pulled her back into Sophie's room.

"I'm fine," Sophie said.

"You look like garbage!" Mary's eyes were wide as she pointed at Sophie. "What happened to your face? It's all wrong."

Her mother chuckled. "You actually look better than I expected. I need to call your mom as soon as we talk to the doctors."

"Then can I go home with Esther and go to my house to play video games on my seventy-two-inch television?"

Mary stomped her foot. "You're grounded, Soapie Eats!"

Esther's mother smiled and patted Sophie's hand. "No, but you can lie on the couch and watch movies with Esther and Nephi, while you sip on 7-up and eat soda crackers."

Sophie fell back on her pillow. "I'm doomed."

Chapter Eleven

Impressions

Esther was used to floating through the halls of Oceanside High alongside Sophie without being noticed. This morning was different. Even though Sophie had only missed school last Friday, everything had changed. She was now the subject of small-town gossip.

"Hi, Sophie." Raquel Owens's heavily made-up face was pulled into a frown as she passed the girls and adjusted her haute couture backpack.

Jackson, their quiet friend and an artist, slipped Sophie a handdrawn card with a hilarious picture of Edna the Medic wheeling Sophie down the hall to the ambulance. He held it out, and she took it and thanked him without stopping to talk. The bell would ring any minute.

"I hope people get onto somebody else's drama soon," Sophie said.

"Welcome to our small town." Esther pushed her glasses up and smiled as they rounded the corner to the administrative office.

Paisley Stuart, Parker's twin and their friend, ran towards them, waving both arms. "Sophie!" She scooped Sophie's short body up and hugged her so hard her feet lifted from the floor. "We were so worried!"

"I'm fine. I slept off and on all weekend, while Esther fed my fish and walked my dog. You haven't lived until you've eaten charcoal and . . ."

"Sophie!" Esther stopped her.

Paisley laughed her deep laugh. "I wanted to bring you chicken soup, but when I tried to make it, I realized I had never made soup before. So, I bought you something else." She handed Sophie a card in a mint green envelope. It matched Paisley's mint green shirt.

"I see we have changed favorite colors," Sophie said.

"Oh, you know me." Paisley beamed and winked. "I love making the world a better place. I am going to pick you two up after school for some fun."

Esther bit her lip. "We have a lot to do after school. Mom and Papa J worked all weekend, and we need to talk to them about Simon."

"Then we'll go with you." She smiled and hugged Esther again. "I'll pick you up at the west doors." Paisley waved goodbye.

"She doesn't take no for an answer," Sophie said.

"And I love that about her." Esther smiled and opened the glass door to the main office. When the door closed, the sounds of the chaos in the halls was muffled.

Their friend Bridget, Madison Merriweather's daughter, was at the counter. She worked an hour a day in the office as a student aid. She wore her usual black shirt and was hunched over the computer. She beamed and came to the counter when she saw Sophie. Sophie held out a note, excusing her from school for being ill.

Bridget tucked her pencil behind her ear and took the note. "You know you don't have to do this now. It's all online." She smiled and began creating a handwritten pink pass for Sophie.

"No, I didn't know. This is the first time I've missed school." Sophie shrugged.

"This year?" Bridget asked.

"Ever." Sophie gave her a cheesy grin. "I like getting a perfect attendance award every year. This is going to ruin my collection."

"My mom thinks someone tried to hurt you," Bridget said softly and glanced over her shoulder to make sure no one else heard.

"Me?" Sophie whispered, pointing at herself. "Why?"

"Probably because she is an author, and you know how they are— all drama and imagination out of control. I've caught her talking to her characters like they are standing in the room. She keeps her own action figures on her desk now, so she doesn't look so cray-cray when she talks to them." Bridget giggled and tucked her pencil into her messy bun, knocking loose a hank of long black hair.

Sophie smiled back. "I love your mom."

Bridget leaned over the counter and said softly, "She wants you to come to the workout today so she can talk to you both and to your mom, Esther. She asked me to come find you at school and tell you to be careful."

Sophie rolled her eyes. "Okay. But I'm fine. Really."

Bridget snickered. "I'm sure you are."

When they arrived at the library, Esther pushed the doors open and froze.

Sophie ran into her back. "Oof."

Esther took another step into the library and let go of the swinging doors.

"Hey." Sophie caught them just as they closed on her.

"Sorry." Esther turned around and tried to get past Sophie and back out of the library doors.

"Esther?" Ms. Priest said. "Welcome back, Sophie. Girls, I want you to meet Jax. He's going to be working in the library with us for the first hour of the day three times a week."

Jax's face broke into a grin, making his dark brown eyes twinkle. He had a nice smile, with beautiful white teeth. His skin was smooth, unlike most high school boys, and he was dressed more like a college student than a high schooler. He had on a patterned button-up shirt tucked into jeans that looked like they were ironed. Esther noticed he wore hiking boots and a backpack clearly labeled with the logo of a famous mountain climbing sports store.

"Aren't you the girls that throw up?" He laughed.

Esther's jaw clenched, and she frowned, but she didn't answer.

"Sorry. I shouldn't laugh. But you should have seen your face when I walked in on you losing your lunch in the library garbage can." He was still smiling.

"I'm glad you enjoyed it." She brushed past him without looking at him. After stashing her backpack under the counter, she hung up her cardigan.

"Dude. Aren't you the music teacher's son?" Sophie said. "You're almost as tall as Esther's uncle, Nephi. That will be handy for shelving books." She joined Esther behind the counter and put away her things.

"I was hoping that you two could show Jax around," Ms. Priest said.

"I'm busy," Esther said. Ms. Priest squinted at her and raised an eyebrow. Esther glanced away and tried to busy herself unlocking the drawer.

"I can do it. Put your gear away here, sasquatch." Sophie pointed at the space behind the desk. "The first thing we are going to teach you is how to shelve books and carry them up the stairs."

"Isn't Esther going to help?" Jax asked. The corner of his mouth twitching as he subdued a smile.

"Just you and me, giant. Now let's get moving."

He walked past Esther, and the most heavenly scent floated with him.

This is going to ruin the library . . .

It was raining when Nephi pulled Paisley's car up to the library's west door. Sophie and Esther ran for the car.

"I can't believe you're letting him drive your car," Esther said.

"Hey," Sophie said. "You're cheating on us. You're our chauffeur."

He smiled and continued chewing his gum. "Trust me. I'm a great driver." He started the car and hit the first speed bump in the parking lot so hard Esther bounced up sideways, almost hitting her head on the car window.

"Slow down!" Esther braced herself for the second speed bump. He stopped and slowly rolled over it.

"Your mom is with our moms," Paisley said. "So, I am going to take you up to the stone church."

"Wait a minute," Sophie said. "This is a trap. Aren't they working out up there? Are you wearing a mint green jogging suit?"

Paisley flashed her bright white teeth and winked at Sophie. Laughing musically, she bounced hard as Nephi went over another speed bump before the highway.

The stone church was nestled in tall pines on the last road up the mountain. There were small houses and duplexes nearby, but the final tenth of a mile was a gravel road to a parking lot.

The church was built sometime in the late 1800s and fit into nature as if it had grown there. It had a deep, covered porch to keep the parishioners dry. The double doors had stained glass windows and were both held open by large rocks. Inside, the main room was emptied of chairs. The parish often rented out the quaint space for meetings and parties. The vaulted ceilings, rough cut beams, beautiful windows, and massive fireplace made it a favorite wedding spot, which created a lucrative income for the congregation. Madison, Mrs. Stuart, Bridget, Grandma Mable, and Grace, Esther's mom, were gathered around the fireplace in their workout gear. Mary was attempting a cartwheel in the center of the empty room.

"Mom?" Esther said.

Her mother turned to look at her and smiled. "I was hoping you'd join us. You're going to love this."

"I am still feeling a little queasy," Sophie said.

"Right. Well, you can sit this one out," Esther's mom said.

"Traitor," Esther whispered to Sophie's smiling face. "Mom, we need to talk, it's important."

"Can't it wait until after class?"

"Sure. We'll go home with Nephi," Esther said.

"He left already. You might as well stay and exercise." Her mother patted her back and walked over to a speaker on the floor, hooked up her phone, and music started thumping and rattling the windows.

"All right ladies! Line up," Melissa Stewart bellowed over the music.

Sophie smiled. Esther would have heard her laughing if the music hadn't been so loud.

"Warm up! March in place. One, two, three . . ."

Esther dropped her backpack by the wall and joined the older women and her friends.

Forty-five minutes later Esther was lying on a yoga mat with her eyes closed, and hands resting palms up at her side, drifting off to sleep. "Ding." The clear ring of brass yoga bells jolted Esther and she sat up.

"Sit up slowly when you're ready." Mrs. Stuart sat, crossing her legs in an impossible way. Meditation music played. Mrs. Stuart looked serene.

She isn't even sweating. She's amazing. Mom? Not so much.

Esther's mom, Grace, rolled on her side and pushed her sweaty blonde curls out of her face. Her hair tie was tangled in a knot of hair on the back of her head. Sweat poured off her face and stained her tight shirt everywhere, including the center of her back. She pushed herself up onto her hands and knees. She knelt and then struggled to half standing, half limp doll, head hanging down, chest heaving for air.

"Doing great!" Grandma Mable smacked her mother on the back, making her cough uncontrollably.

"Grandma Mable, you aren't even glistening. You're a rock!" Sophie gathered her homework up and put it back in her backpack.

"Mom, we really need to talk."

Grace was still bent over with her hands on her knees, catching her breath. She held up one finger. "Just . . . a . . . . minute."

Esther lowered her voice and leaned closer to her mother's curly hair. "It's about Simon."

Grace's head snapped up, and she stood up. Gulping one more lungful of air, she said, "Okay. What about Simon?" Her eyes narrowed, and she tipped her head, studying Esther like every suspicious mother of a teenager. She put her hands on her hips. "Well. Go on."

"Not here."

"Why not here? We all know Simon." Her mom's last sentence was loud enough that it echoed in the room, bringing the others over to see what was happening.

"Mom!"

"Esther. Just say it."

"We're sure Simon's death wasn't an accident," Esther said, holding back the important piece of information, the paper they'd taken from Simon's hand.

Her mother chuckled. "I know you think that. Lately, we've had a lot of drama in this little town. It's made you suspicious."

"And we took evidence from the scene," Sophie said loudly. Now everyone was silent and staring at them. Esther looked at the floor.

"Evidence?" Madison said. She stepped closer to Sophie. "What evidence? I am gravely concerned for your safety. What if someone tried to poison you because of what you took from the scene. Why didn't I see you there?"

Sophie pushed her glasses up and stuck out her chin, looking fearless. "We were there. He had a picture of Esther in his hand. There was a message on the back of the picture, so we took it and took photos of him, the stage and everything. Videos too."

"You took videos of a dead body?" Bridget asked. "Cool."

"Sophie! Esther!" Her mother's mouth fell open.

Madison swung around to face Bridget. "I may write books about murder, but we still respect the sanctity of life." She turned her back to Bridget and asked Sophie. "Where is the picture?"

Sophie fished around in her pack. "It's right . . . I have it. Just a minute." She looked down in the large bag and pulled out a wrinkled piece of paper. "Here."

The whole room was silent. Esther looked from surprised face to surprised face. The only person that seemed calm was Madison Merriweather.

Madison took the paper from Sophie's hand and unfolded it. "Grace, do you know when this photo of Esther was taken?" She held up the picture.

"That's her school photo from last year." Her mom reached out and took the paper.

"The words *The End* are written on the back in pencil," Sophie said.

Madison reached out and Grace gave her back the paper. "The words are all caps. Does anyone recognize the handwriting?" She held it up. Everyone shook their heads. "Grace, I suspect that the girls are in serious danger. I believe they saw something. They're right. Simon was murdered. I wish they had tested Sophie at the hospital. I don't think she had food poisoning because the only other person to get sick was the counselor, and he was back at school the next morning. I've looked at the event and I can't deduce who has organized it."

Esther's mother frowned. "Well, one thing is for sure. You girls aren't going." She folded the paper and looked at Madison.

Madison talked with her hands. "I have this feeling. When Simon died, Bob the janitor was taking me to see Simon and the auditorium. We were the first on the scene, except for Mephisto. I know I went down pretty fast, but Mephisto was doing something on stage with his back to us. When I came to, he was touching the ladder that Simon supposedly fell off of. So, the police didn't see the actual murder scene. I called the medical examiner, but she said a feeling isn't enough of a reason to do an autopsy and since I'm not Miss Marple, my opinion doesn't count."

"I can't believe she said that!" Melissa Stuart gasped and put her hand over her mouth. "She obviously doesn't know who you are."

"Who am I? I'm just an author." Madison frowned.

"Well, as much as I trust your instincts, I am not sure the police will." Esther's mom shrugged. "Where would Simon have found this photo?"

"There are old yearbooks upstairs in the library. Maybe he or Bob made copies in the conference room while they were working," Esther said. "Anyone can find a yearbook or look up the photos online. The newspaper prints the entire school's yearbook photos every year when school gets out."

"There's more," Sophie said. "Someone posted a photo of the place that Ashley's body was found on the event page for *The End*, with a caption that reads, 'Remember the good times.' Here I'll show you." Sophie scrolled through social media. "It's gone. Yesterday there was a picture of a ladder and a picture of the body, but they didn't stay up long. Then there was a picture of us on the stage like someone was behind the curtains when we were there."

"Did you save any of them?" Esther's mother asked.

Sophie shook her head. "I should have screenshot them as soon as I saw them."

"Sophie, tell us exactly what happened and don't leave anything out," Madison said.

"Well, Esther and I were in the library when we realized that without an amazing community service project we weren't going to get accepted at any colleges. So, I thought of this really great idea."

"Sophie," Esther said.

"No. Let her go on," Madison said.

Esther shifted her weight and wished she could lay back down for the rest of Sophie's story.

"See, we help you with your one act play by acting as stagehands, marketing the play, organizing and gathering props, costumes, you know? Then, Bridget will be sure to be a part of planning which will look good on her college application. And she stars as the singer in the play."

"That's a brilliant idea!" Madison grinned and clapped her hands.

"See! I've been trying to tell everyone . . ."

"Sophie," Esther's mom said. "Continue."

Several minutes later, Sophie wrapped the story up. "That's when Jax, Mr. Phelps's son walked in and saw Esther ralphing in the circular file." Sophie laughed and everyone joined her except Esther, who rolled her eyes and touched her hot cheeks.

"Okay, okay. It's been a week of grossness," Esther said.

"It was a ralph-o-rama," Sophie said. "That charcoal was interesting."

"About how long between the time you ingested the donut and when you threw up?" Madison asked.

"I don't know. Maybe fifteen minutes? Longer?"

"And you say Mephisto was sick too?"

"Yes. I was a lot sicker, but I am smaller, you know? It takes food poisoning less time to do its damage in a short person." Sophie shrugged and held her hands out. "Weight and metabolism would affect anything ingested."

"How sick was Mephisto? Did he buy the donuts?" Madison asked, her brows gathered, and her eyes narrowed.

"He bought them from the new kid, Jax, at the Sweet Stop Bakery. Mephisto sort of threw up a little. Just white powder mostly. Then he must have put the donut box in the garbage," Sophie said.

Madison stood up and pointed at Sophie. "You and me. We need to give this some serious thought. Tomorrow after school, you girls come and meet Bridget and I in the cafeteria, and we'll plan the play and talk this over."

Sophie nodded. "As soon as the bell rings, we'll be there."

Her mother zipped up her hoodie. "Well, we need to get home. We'll talk more about this with Papa J. Thanks, ladies, we will see you in the morning. I need to call Sophie's mom tonight. Her mother wondered if she should come home early, and I talked her out of it. She should know everything."

Esther and Sophie rode silently in the back seat of her mother's SUV. They had tried to talk to her mother, but she used sign language to indicate Mary was listening, and to wait. "She's heard enough tonight. She's going to have nightmares."

"Or grow up to be a great detective," Sophie said.

Esther's mother made a zipping motion across her lips and used her mom face to end the conversation.

The sun had set. The streetlamps were on. They rounded the last corner and parked in front of Esther's house on the curb. Down the street the sky was lit up with flashing red, blue, and amber lights. Three squad cars were parked in front of Sophie's house.

"What's going on?" Sophie leaned over the front seat.

"I don't know, but you girls take Mary inside and wait for me," Esther's mom said.

Esther and Sophie got out and gathered their things while Mary ran up the porch stairs to Mable, who stood with the new neighbor, Marion, watching the commotion down the street.

"What happened, Grandma?" Esther set everything down inside the front door and joined Sophie and Grandma Mable. Mary sat in the porch swing and rocked furiously.

"Maybe it's a fire?" Mary said.

Esther heard a sharp intake of breath and watched Sophies eyes grow rounder.

"The lab . . ." Sophie said. She ran down the stairs, with Esther right on her heels.

"Sophie! Sophie, wait up!"

She didn't stop. Esther's mother was standing behind the squad cars talking to Ironpot, who spotted the girls and used his considerable size to get between them and Sophie's house.

"Whoa, Sophie. Girls stop." He held both hands up in front of them and motioned for them to come to him.

"I need to make sure the lab is secure. It has combustibles in it, you know—volatile compounds." Sophie raised her hands and made the sound of an explosion.

"Sophie, I know we've known each other a long time and I work with Esther's stepdad and mom so you know me as their friend, but this is one rule I can't break for anyone. Even someone I know as well as I know you, Esther, and her mom," Ironpot said.

"What about Spam, my dog?" Sophie's fists clenched, her eyes were wide with worry and pooling with rare tears.

Ironpot looked at the house, looked back at Sophie and trotted over to one of the other officers. He wiped his brow and returned. "No one got in the lab."

Sophie stared at officers going in and out of the front door. "The area rugs are white. They should take their shoes off."

Ironpot chuckled. "I'll let them know."

"What happened?" Sophie asked.

"We've already talked to your folks. They were on the speakers and security cameras when we arrived. The alarms went off alerting us at the station. They could see the intruder on camera, but he wore black and had his face covered. Whoever broke in, came in through a window on the beach side. When they broke it, it sent us a notification, and we arrived within a few minutes."

"Did you have your sirens on?" Esther asked.

"We were code three. Yes. We didn't know who was in the house. Sophie could have been home alone." Ironpot shrugged. "People's safety comes before sneaking up on bad guys."

Esther nodded but couldn't take her eyes off the officers talking to each other, coming, and going, and making notes.

"We don't think anything was taken but it's impossible to tell. It looks like they tried the code on the lab door, and when it wouldn't work, they smashed the pad. It still didn't open. It was amateur hour. They emptied drawers and tossed closets, throwing everything on the floor. It's a mess."

"I wonder what they wanted?" Sophie said.

"That's just it. It's messy enough, we aren't sure what they were looking for. Let me see if the chief will let you walk through the house to see if you notice anything missing." He radioed in using the mic clipped to his shoulder. He had an earpiece on, so they couldn't hear the response. "He's going to talk to the other officers and let them know. Wait right here."

"Are you all right?" Esther searched Sophie's blank face.

"I'm furious," Sophie growled and balled her hands into fists.

Ironpot came back and motioned for Grace and the girls to join him. "Don't touch anything. If you want something moved, let me know." He held up gloved hands.

"Spam! I've got to find Spam!" Sophie said.

"Spam?" Ironpot scratched his forehead.

"Our Shih Tzu. His name is Spam."

He shook his head, shrugged. "I am so sorry. I didn't think about your dog. No one has seen a dog yet."

He motioned for the girls to follow him. They wove through the patrol cars and officers.

"Follow me, exactly. Don't go off on your own." Ironpot wiped his feet on the door mat.

"Thank you." Sophie took her shoes off and set them under the bamboo bench by the door. She quietly picked up a potted plant that was knocked down and set back up.

The breeze from the broken window traveled through the house and blew Esther's hair out of her face. "Burr, it's cold tonight."

Ironpot walked to the hallway off the living room. "There is a local clean up company. Your folks called them. As soon as we clear the scene, they will clean up the house and cover the window until it can be replaced. It isn't as bad as it looks."

"Isn't it?" Sophie said. "You don't know my parents. Dust doesn't live here. They don't allow it."

Drawers were opened. Papers were everywhere. Sophie stopped at a tall glass table with a mirror over it. She touched the green statue on top of the table. "This is an extremely valuable jade statue my parents picked up in their travels before I was born." Her head snapped up, and she ran down the hall into her parent's room and fell down on the floor, pulling a box out from underneath the bed. "Phew! It's my parent's important papers, and my Grandma Ito's wedding rings, and other valuables. They could have walked out the door with it." She sat back down on the floor with the portable safe in her lap.

Esther heard whimpering coming from behind the closet door. She slid the door open and saw Spam's big eyes looking back at her. The poor dog was trembling.

"Spam!" Sophie opened her arms and leaned forward. The dog jumped into her arms, vibrating. "It's alright, buddy. It's okay. Let's go home and brush your hair." She took a sweater off a hanger and wrapped the dog with it. They continued their search of the house.

After they had walked through the rest of the house, they met with Ironpot on the front lawn.

Esther carried a large diaper bag full of doggie diapers, brushes, a dog basket, and Spam's sterling silver food and water dishes.

Sophie lovingly carried the quivering dog, reassuring him like a new baby with a gold bow in its hair.

"Well?" Ironpot held a flipbook in his hands and a pen poised for notes. "What's missing?"

"I can't see a thing, unless my parents had important papers I don't know about. The lab is still secure, thankfully."

"We thought so. Your mom and dad searched the rooms using the security cameras. Creepy. I'm telling you. Seriously, *1984*."

"Pardon me?" Esther asked.

"You probably don't know the book. It was banned years before you were born." Ironpot said. "Did you watch the movie?"

Esther looked at Sophie, looked at him, and said, "Never heard of it."

Grace laughed. She patted Ironpot on the arm. "Getting old, Potty. Getting old."

Esther held the door open for Sophie and Spam.

Mary ran toward the dog. "Spam!"

Sophie held one hand out like a stop sign and sheltered Spam with her other arm. "Hold it, Goober. Spam is scared."

"Can we turn down the lights?" Esther said.

Mable turned the lights off, leaving one lamp lit. A fire warmed the room. Esther noticed another letter from her father on the little table by the door that held mail and car keys. *Odd. Two in a short time? Get a grip. The last thing I need is his drama. I can't even think about him right now.*

Papa J came out of the kitchen wearing a red polka dot apron that said, *Kiss the Cook.* It was covered in marinara sauce and flour. "I made some homemade pizza. I talked to Ironpot earlier, and I thought you might enjoy some comfort food. No salads for dinner. It will be ready in ten minutes."

Esther sat the dog basket by the fireplace where Miss Molly was enjoying the warm hearth. Sophie unwrapped Spam. Miss Molly spotted Spam, arched her back, and hissed.

Esther reached out, "It's okay, Molly." She tried to pick her up. Miss Molly's claws dug into her sweater as she jumped out of Esther's arms and ran for the stairs, no doubt going to her favorite hiding spot under Esther's bed.

"Sophie, are you okay?" Nephi came in the front door. "Parker and I were working on the van earlier with Papa J when we heard about the break in."

Sophie knelt on the floor next to Spam's basket and gently brushed his hair.

Nephi sat down by the dog. "Hey, you brought me a chicken nugget." Spam brightened up, left the basket, and climbed into Nephi's lap, putting his paws on his chest and trying to lick his face. When he couldn't reach it, he pawed his chest until Nephi leaned down for a wet dog kiss.

"Sorry." Sophie blushed and tried to pick Spam up. Spam wriggled out of her hands and made himself comfortable in Nephi's lap.

Esther's mom came in the front door. "I finally talked to your parents. Your grandma had surgery this morning. I told them we were fine, and that Spam could stay here. Let's try not to worry them. They have a lot on their mind."

"Mom, what if Madison is right and Sophie is in danger?" Esther asked.

"Let's not get paranoid. Sophie's father thinks they may have been looking for one of the projects he's trying to patent." Esther's mom put her coat on a hook and walked stiffly to the couch. "I'm so sore."

"What is he making?" Nephi asked.

"He wouldn't say. He said he doesn't want anyone to find out until he has the patent," Esther's mom said, and then flopped back on the couch, and tried to straighten her hair.

"He's been working on hydropower. Mom wants to make home windmills a true reality for green energy and off-grid living. But Dad's main focus is on battery storage systems and semiconductors. If Dad's successful, he says we can buy a bigger lab, or at least go down five more levels." Sophie smiled. "I get to help him once he has the designs for his projects protected."

"Nice!" Nephi said. "I've been reading about hydropower. Did you know that although it's renewable and reliable energy source that looks green, there are still serious questions about how it impacts the environment? There are suggestions that fish and soil around hydro-plants located in the ocean are impacted negatively."

"Who are you and what have you done with Nephi?" Esther said.

"You aren't the only geek. I like science stuff." Nephi used Sophie's brush and gently detangled Spam's long hair.

"Where's Parker?" Esther asked.

"He had to head home to finish some homework before tomorrow," Nephi said.

"Dinner's ready," Mable called from the other room.

"I get the red chair!" Mary ran into the kitchen.

"I'll be right there." Esther's mother struggled to get up. Esther finally stood over her and helped her up.

"I thought exercise was supposed to make you stronger and be good for you," Esther said.

"Listen, Little Miss Smarty Pants, a few more weeks of Melissa's classes and I might try out for the Navy Seals." Her mom shuffled ahead of her towards the smell of pizza, hot out of the oven. Esther heard her say, "Love me, Hart. Rub my shoulders and feed me."

"Come eat, Sophie," Nephi said. "I'll carry Spam. I've been think-ing. I think Madison is right and you shouldn't be alone. This is twice that you've come way too close to being hurt. Spam and I are going to go rogue and be your bodyguards. If we don't get this figured out soon, Spam could end up being an orphan and we can't have that."

After dinner, Esther helped Sophie pack Spam's bag and basket up to her bedroom. Carrying her backpack full of books and Spam's bag up two flights of stairs winded her. She stopped at the top for a moment and let Sophie go first. When they reached her bedroom, Sophie gently let Spam down. His nails marked every step as he pranced toward Esther's double bed.

Then before Esther could stop Spam, he made a break for under her bed. She could hear Miss Molly warn him with a low meow and half growl. Spam yipped. She heard Molly hiss and then a painful yelp. Spam ran out from under her bed to Sophie, who dropped her load and caught him on the first leap. Molly's growl let everyone in earshot know how she felt about sharing her private sanctuary.

"What are we going to do?" Sophie asked.

Laying on her belly, Esther tried to reach Molly, cooing, kissing, and begging in the dust bunnies. But Molly just turned her nose up. She was the one betrayed and was going to make sure Esther knew what she thought about Spam being in her room.

Esther heard a deep chuckle and looked over her shoulder at Nephi's massive converse high tops. "You think you can do any better?"

"Come here, buddy. We men have to stick together." Above her head, the bed bowed and threatened to squish her. Molly passed her on a dead run, her nails skittering across the floor as she tried to turn and make it out of the door. Esther moved to the side and pushed her dusty body out from under the bed. She rolled over and flopped on her back next to the bed.

"I can't move. Mrs. Stuart tried to kill us," Esther said.

"I hear she is pretty good. Not as good as I am, but hey—not everyone can be me." Nephi winked at Sophie.

"Thank heavens." Esther rolled onto her stomach. "What are you doing up here?"

A rare cloud of emotion passed across Nephi's usually sunny face. He frowned, and sighed, looking down. "For once I agree with

Madison, one-hundred percent." He looked up and stared intensely at Sophie. "I think, for some reason, someone wants you out of the way. You may not even know why. But two brushes with death in two days is two too many and it infuriates me."

Sophie sat down hard on Esther's rocking chair. Her mouth fell open. "You don't think it's just a coincidence?"

He scratched Spam behind his ears. "Not at all. Look, you heard Simon and Lars London talking. You told us in the garage. London wants to get rid of the library and maybe the whole building. He is always looking to make a buck. What if he killed Simon and thinks you saw him?"

"Maybe," Sophie said. "But that doesn't explain the donuts. Jax is a wild card. He made the donuts, and he's new in town."

"He doesn't strike me as a killer," Esther said, rubbing her neck.

"Whoa. What have we here?" Sophie snickered. "One minute you treat him like he has the plague and the next you're defending him?"

Nephi laughed. "Who is Jax? Does Parker know he has competition?"

Esther pulled off a dirty sock and threw it at Nephi, who ducked. "Not funny. He is just the new music teacher's son. Jax? You've seen him? Tall like you, short black hair, and really brown eyes with flecks of gold?"

"Flecks of gold?" Nephi laughed loud and long. "You got it bad! I suppose he's smart too."

"I do not!" She sent the other sock in his direction.

Sophie smiled and rocked the rocking chair. When the laughter died down, she looked at Nephi and said, "What would Jax's motive be? He doesn't even know me. Why me?"

"Maybe he's crazy. Maybe he just looks nice, but Esther is done with handsome and kind and is moving onto certifiable? You know, the nice guy who turns out to be a serial killer?"

"Har, har," Esther said. "Seriously, he drives me nuts." That started a new round of laughter.

Esther's mom poked her head in the door. She had dark circles under her eyes, and her lean body was slumped. She pushed her matted hair out of her face. "Keep it down. Nephi, you need to let the girls have some privacy. It's time to shut things down. Everyone needs some sleep."

"It's barely eight o'clock," Nephi said. "We still have time for a movie."

Esther's mom looked at her. "It's only eight? That means we only have ten hours until our 7 a.m. run with Melissa. I'm going to die. Aren't you tired? Seriously?" She held out the letters from downstairs.

"Throw them away, Mom. I can't handle him or his letters right now. Mephisto says I don't have to answer him or even be involved with him. I should just take care of myself. You do you and I do me."

"I'll keep them until you ask for them. Even if it's never." Her mom smiled sadly and went down the hall to her room. "Hart? Rub my feet."

"That's disgusting," Sophie said.

Nephi chuckled. "I want my feet rubbed."

"I don't have a hazmat suit." Sophie smiled. "Anyway, you were saying—Jax? What is the motive? Maybe he's jealous of my friendship with Esther? After all, I sense a little crush between you two."

"Seriously? Knock it off." Esther started trying to stretch out her legs. "Okay. Back to Simon. Sophie, I hate to say it, but I agree with Nephi and Madison. Something is seriously wrong, and you seem to be a target. It all began with the library argument and Simon's death. I'm afraid if we don't figure it out before *The End*, it may be *our* end. We have to do this. And if we don't figure it out before the event, then we have to go to *The End* to see who's behind it, while trying to keep everyone else from going."

"So, you agree, the event, Simon's death, and what's happened to Sophie are connected?" Nephi asked.

"It's time for a murder board. We need to know what all these things have in common and which ones are just coincidence," Sophie said.

"I don't believe in coincidence," Esther and Nephi said at the same time.

"Jinx," they both said.

"I'm so tired from working out, I can't think," Esther said.

Nephi smiled. "Grace is right. It's time for bed. I'll take Spam with me so Miss Molly can come back and sleep on your bed. We'll bunk on the couch in the living room. No one is getting past Papa J or me. Let's sleep on it."

"If I sleep," Sophie said. "Spam—you traitor. Don't smile at me like that." Spam licked Nephi's face.

Chapter Twelve

Organic Reach

The last bell rang loud and long. Jax opened the double doors, letting the sound follow him into the library. The bell stopped, Jax smiled at Esther and Sophie while the heavy wooden doors swung back and forth behind him until they closed.

"Is Ms. Priest here?" He gave them a blinding smile. "My dad wanted to invite her to the meeting."

"The meeting? Which meeting?" Esther said.

"You know. Madison's. Right now, here, in the library." He was still smiling as he leaned comfortably across the counter and rested on his elbows. "You're coming too. Right?"

Esther's mouth hung open. "I . . . ah . . ."

Sophie patted Esther on the back. "We didn't know it was a community meeting. We were hoping for a small planning party."

"I'm here." Ms. Priest came out of her office. "I plan on attending. I am fully invested in putting our historic auditorium and library to good use. We need to remind the entire community that they are a treasure we can't afford to neglect."

"Speak it!" Sophie pumped her fist in the air.

"Hello, lovelies." Madison blew into the library through the west doors, with Bridget and her guitar following.

Doctor Phelps, Jax's father, was right behind Madison, with his head down and his hands in the pockets of another tweed jacket. He patted his son on the back.

Bob, the janitor, pushed through the school doors in a brown shirt.

"Whoa, Bob. You lost the red shirt," Sophie said.

He shrugged. "We all know what happens to the guy in the red shirt. They are expendable and die in every Star Trek episode."

Mrs. Stuart came in the west door at the same time as the twins, Paisley and Parker. Nephi held Paisley's hand. "Well," Mrs. Stuart said, "It looks like the gang's all here!"

"We can't fail with a winning team like this." Madison clapped her hands and waved them over to the fireplace. She flicked the gas flame on and settled into a deep leather sofa.

Madison's joyful face fell as she pawed through her large purse. "I have everything I need to get us organized." She began pulling papers out and a small laptop.

"Here," Paisley said. "Let me help you." She gathered up Madison's stack of papers, and quickly looked through them, and separated them into piles, like a Vegas card shark with very large cards.

"Thank you." Madison patted the couch next to her and Paisley sat down on her left while Bridget sat on her right. "My Bridget and I have created a fun little one act play for Doctor Phelps to direct. It's based on a book I wrote before I was ever published. The play takes place in one location in the forest. The actors are magical and live among the trees. Our new Stone Circle Park is the perfect location to stage it. It is a sort of Romeo and Juliet, only the families are Fae or mythical little fairies or pixies. It all has a very ancient Scottish feel to it. Right, my dear?" She smiled at Bridget. "Oh! And of course, a happy ending. I also have some talent visiting to warm everyone up with a mini-concert."

Bridget's alabaster skin turned bright pink. She looked at the floor.

"Is Bridget willing to sing in it?" Esther asked.

"Bridget?" Madison held her breath and looked at her daughter, waiting quietly for her to answer. Bridget just nodded. Madison exhaled in relief, looked up, smiled and said to the group, "You can't wait. I promise you."

"I love your voice, Bridget," Esther said. She smiled and tried to wink, but to her eternal frustration, she could only blink both eyes. "We'll be there with you."

"Scout's honor," Sophie said.

Bridget looked up and chuckled. "Jax is the lead. I sing, but he does too."

Madison looked at Esther. "Esther, I know you wanted to help organize, but I was hoping you would also play a key part in the play."

Esther cleared her throat. "Shouldn't we have auditions? Maybe Sophie or Paisley want the part?" Esther said.

Paisley held one hand up, like she was stopping traffic. "Oh, no! I am not getting on stage. I am happy to organize, but I don't want all that pressure." She looked from face to face with wide eyes. "I just want to organize the thing. If I go to college, that's plenty for my application."

"Me too," Bridget said quietly.

Madison melted. "You don't have to do anything, Bridget. Maybe this just isn't the right time. We only have a few weeks to put it together for the holidays and before the weather gets unbearable. Maybe it's too much."

Sophie jumped up, making her as tall as everyone who was seated. "Stop the train! We can totally do this." She scanned the room. "Bridget, you know we all love listening to you sing. Please? Maybe none of you care, but I do."

Parker chuckled. "We can do another project, Sophie."

Sophie deflated and fell back onto the couch. Esther noticed Bridget was watching her closely. Then Bridget looked at Jax. Jax's mouth was actually turned down. Even his eyes looked sad. He picked at the frayed cuff of his shirt. Mr. Phelps's arms were folded tightly. Esther couldn't tell how he felt. He had on small round glasses that masked his expression.

Doctor Phelps needs the work. Look at his shirt.

Esther scooted forward in her seat. "I'll do it. I'll do it on two conditions. If the proceeds go to a scholarship in Simon's name and if you will, Bridget, I will. I agree with Sophie. Your voice is magical, and I want to be there the first time the world hears you sing."

Bridget's lips were pressed into a straight, expressionless line. Her gaze ping-ponged between her mother and Esther. Then she looked at Jax again. "I'll do it." Her voice was so soft it was swallowed up in Sophie's cheer.

"You won't regret it, Bridget." Her mother smiled, and Bridget moved closer and sat at her feet. Madison leaned over and kissed her on the forehead. "We can be brave together. And Esther, that's an excellent idea. We can begin the Simon Memorial Scholarship Fund."

The room relaxed. Doctor Phelps stood up and for the first time Esther heard him speak. "I will post a practice schedule. There are very few parts, but we will need to hold a small audition quickly. Bob, I'll coordinate the schedule with you, so the building is open when we need it." His voice was like butter melting on toast. It was smooth and yet carried in a commanding way. He seemed like a gentle and kind man.

Bob nodded and pulled out a small pencil and pad. He wrote down a note. "No problem. I am still learning Simon's job, but I think that's okay."

Simon's name shot through Esther's heart like an arrow.

Doctor Phelps gave Bob a sad smile. "Can we meet first thing in the morning? And let's all get back together tomorrow, same time, same place. Paisley, can you come meet me at lunch? And Parker, plan on auditioning."

"I'll run the stage lights and help with scenery," Nephi said. Paisley gave him a kiss, leaving her lipstick on his cheek and a silly grin on his face.

"Perfect!" Madison stood up and applauded. "Now, Melissa. Let's go work out."

Bridget put her face in her hands and groaned audibly. "Do we have to?"

"Not at all. Maybe you and Jax could practice the love song you wrote."

Sophie snickered. Jax's head whipped around. "What's so funny."
"Nothing," Sophie said and stifled another giggle. Bridget's face was flushed again.

"Mom, is it okay if I go home with Nephi?" Paisley asked. "I need to walk Cornwallis and feed him. Nephi can keep me company."

"You're going to miss our workout." Her mom frowned. "Will you run with us in the morning?"

"Promise." Paisley kissed her mom and gathered her things. "I'll make us a fruit and yogurt when I get home." Her mother hugged her, smiling.

Parker stood up and offered Esther his hand and helped her up. "Can I give you a lift to Chez James Garage? I hear they serve charcuterie boards."

"They're to die for," Esther said.

Sophie gave her a playful push. "Not funny, E. Not funny. Shotgun!"

Parker rolled the garage door up, looking like he was at home.

A cat skittered out of the garage as soon as the door was opened.

"Oh, there you are, Benny!" Marion J. Herbert, the new neighbor, stepped out of the trees lining the parking lot and scooped up the running cat. He was wearing a fluffy robe over his shirt and tie. "I've been looking for you everywhere." He ran his hand through his brown hair and walked closer. "Naughty kitty."

Esther realized her mouth was open and closed it. Her heart was pumping loudly in her ears. "You scared me."

"I am so sorry. Benny got out, and I have been wandering the neighborhood looking for my precious little boy." He tried to hold Benny, who struggled in his arms. "Time to take you home, bad boy. By the way, I haven't seen Mable lately. Is everything okay?"

"Yes. She's just busy with Mary, my little sister. Do you want me to tell her that you asked about her?"

"It's okay. No rush. I'm moving in a roommate at the end of the week. I am so excited about him. He is a licensed music therapist. We'll be able to collaborate and maybe even work together on couples' retreats. He and I are both new to the area. I was hoping Mable would help me find good restaurants and information for his teenage son. Perhaps you've met him? Jax?"

Surprised, Esther said, "He goes to school with us."

"Well, tell Mable that Marion said hello. I am hoping she'll want to go with me to the best coffee shops and tell me what to do for fun in this tiny town." He smiled back. "Well, toodles!"

Esther put her hand over her mouth and wondered why he made her laugh.

Sophie pointed at his retreating form. "See! I've been saying he's creepy. What if he put his own cat in the garage?"

"How did he get in the garage?" Parker said.

"Not a teeny, tiny clue." Esther shrugged and watched Marion disappear in the trees between the houses.

"Creepy infinity," Sophie said. Sophie turned all the lights on.

"Where's Papa J?" Parker asked.

Esther picked up a note off the tool bench. "I don't know, but he left a note and instructions. He says he found someone to paint the van, but first we need to give it one last sanding to save money and make sure it's perfectly smooth."

"I can't sand it any longer." Sophie laughed at her own joke. "What's to eat?"

Parker opened the fridge and looked on the tool bench. "Powdered donuts, apples, and potato chips."

"Yeah, I'm over donuts." Sophie took the bag of chips and pulled it open. "Anyone want a diet soda?" Esther took one.

Esther was opening her soda when Nephi pulled into the driveway. "Let's start with the murder board and then do the van. I can't seem to put all the pieces together. It's like a game of chess with four sides and everyone is moving."

Paisley and Bridget got out of the truck with Nephi. "What's for dinner?"

"Donuts, chips, and soda," Parker said.

"Perfect." Nephi stuffed a donut in his mouth. Sophie gasped and watched him chew it, holding her breath. Nephi slapped her on the back and laughed until white powder blew all over her. "Sorry! I'll toss them and go find something else." He was laughing so hard he started choking on his donut.

"Serves you right, Sasquatch." Sophie rolled her eyes.

"I'll be right back with some food," Nephi said.

Esther found a marker on the tool bench. "There's a bare patch over here." She moved close to the door. "Okay, let's start with Simon." She put Simon's name in the middle of the wall.

"Are you sure we shouldn't start with Sophie's name?" Parker said.

The idea hit Esther in her gut.

"I still think it's coincidence." Sophie opened her soda.

"Queen of de-nile," Parker said. He took the marker from Esther's hand and put Sophie's name in large letters at the top of the board. "No one messes with one of ours."

He stepped back and stood next to Esther. She reached out and put her shaky hand on his arm, looking in his eyes. They both knew she was grateful.

"Okay," Esther said. "Here's the connection I see. We were witnesses at the scene of Simon's death. Sophie must have seen something or have something I didn't see or don't have. Something that created a reason for her to be targeted. We're missing something." She put her name next to Sophie's and drew a solid line between them and a solid line to Simon.

Sophie reached out and Esther handed her the marker. "What about Bob? He's a new face. He got Simon's job."

"A janitor's job is hardly worth killing over." Esther bit her lip. "But Simon was teasing him pretty hard core."

Sophie wrote his name down. "Still, what is the motive? Bad dad jokes?" She drew a dotted line to Simon.

Nephi came back to the garage with Spam in his arms and a jar of trail mix. "This is all I could find, unless you want green salads."

"Thanks, man," Parker said and opened the trail mix.

"Spam, you traitor, back to business. Who had a motive to kill Simon?" Sophie asked. Spam seemed to smile at Sophie and yipped before snuggling deep into Nephi's arms.

"We know Lars London wanted his house, and it had something to do with making money," Esther said. "He might be building another vacation timeshare or development and wants the land that the school and Simon's house are on."

"I think he wants the land the school is on," Bridget said. "I've been listening in on some of Mom's calls to board members. Principal

Kelly has been talking about moving the school to a new and modern building in a tsunami safe zone. You know, up the mountain."

"But we love this one. It's so totally Necanicum," Paisley said. "Our brand is beach, beautiful, and shabby chic. Not stainless steel and glass. Oceanside High fits with Necanicum's quaint beach cottages and Victorian Mansions. The school and the light house are both less than two hundred years old. In Britain, they're practically brand new."

Sophie smiled. "I agree, but my brand is better Wi-Fi and computers. It's time to admit the dinosaurs are extinct, but we're still using the computers they left behind."

"But is that a motive for murder?" Esther said. "What does he stand to lose if he can't have the property?"

"That's a good question," Parker said.

"Who else would have a motive?" Nephi asked. "I can think of a lot of motives to off Sophie, but no one does her in but me. Are we clear?"

Esther picked up another marker and chewed on one end, looking at the board. "Something is missing." She uncapped the marker and in the dead center of the wall she wrote in all caps, *The End* and the outline of a head with a question mark where the face should be.

"Has anyone looked at the event tonight?" Paisley pulled out her phone and started scrolling.

Nephi stroked Spam's soft fur. "What about the creepy neighbor? He knows Sophie. Does he know Simon? Maybe Simon was the accident and Sophie was the actual target?" Nephi leaned over Spam. "We don't like cats, do we, little Spammy Whammy."

Sophie face palmed herself. "You're going to ruin my guard dog."

Nephi chuckled with a look of happy satisfaction. "Well, the creepy neighbor is new in town. So is Jax the donut maker."

"And so is Doctor Phelps. I'm putting them over here." Esther said. "So far I can't make heads or tails of a single thing. Do we need to look more at London or the neighbor? And what about Jax and his dad? What would they have to gain by hurting Simon or Sophie? None of it makes sense. I keep coming back to the event and the threatening posts. Simon died with the photos of *The End* event page in his hands."

"The vaguely threatening posts," Sophie said. "This entire thing is vague. There's a piece we don't have."

"Hey guys," Paisley said, still looking at her phone. "I'm going to screenshot these. Esther, your pictures are here. All of our pictures are here. But there are some faces I don't recognize at all." Everyone pulled their phones out and started scrolling. "Look." Paisley held hers up and there was a photo that looked ragged around the edges with a girl in braids and braces. She had brown hair like Esther's and eyes like Esther's, but she had freckles across her nose. "Does anyone recognize her?"

"I don't," Esther said.

Paisley looked at the picture again. "She could be your twin, just younger and well, not as you. If you know what I mean."

"What about this girl?" Sophie held up a photo. It was another girl with brown braids, like Esther liked to wear, complicated. She didn't have freckles or braces, but she had glasses.

"We have to figure out who these girls are. I am going to screenshot everything." Esther began capturing photos.

"Esther," Papa J said.

Esther's head snapped up. "I didn't hear you come in."

Papa J had his police face on. Expressionless, but his eyes looked sad. "Esther?" He motioned, and her heart dropped. He wanted her to come with him.

"It's okay. We should clean up. I have a ton of homework," Bridget said.

Parker kissed her cheek. He waved as she numbly followed Papa J, and Sophie followed her.

Chapter Thirteen

Lurker

Papa J held the door open for Esther and Sophie. Her mother stood by the fireplace holding an envelope.

"Have a seat," Grace said.

Obediently, Esther and Sophie sat together on the couch.

"I owe you an apology." Her mother bit her lip and stared intensely at Esther.

"Me?" Esther pointed at herself.

Her mom's eyebrows rose, and she ran her hand through her curly hair, once, twice, making it bigger with each stroke. "I've been talking to your dad."

Esther heart jumped. "What? Why . . . I . . .?"

Sophie stared at her, eyes wide behind her glasses, and grimaced.

Her mom took a deep breath and let it out slowly. "I realize now, I should have talked to you first."

"I don't understand. Why would you talk to him? He wrote to me, not you." Letting her words hang in the air, Esther folded her arms tightly.

Her mom looked at the floor, hiding in her long hair. She folded her arms like Esther and looked up. "He called collect. I answered the phone, accepted the call, and we spoke."

"Why?"

"Let me explain."

Esther pushed herself deeper into the couch and studied her feet.

Her mother began to pace. "I don't know why I accepted the charges. When he called, he hadn't written to you yet. He wanted me to ask you to forgive him. I thought about it, but I felt like it wasn't a good idea for me to relay messages to you. If he wanted forgiveness, he needed to ask for himself."

"You told him to write? You're the reason I keep getting letters from prison?" Wrapping her arms tightly around her middle, she folded in on herself.

"I'm sorry, Esther. Will you let me explain? I have to tell you a few more things."

"More?" Sophie said. Her arm slipped around Esther's shoulders.

Her mom sighed. "He wanted to know about you. I know you don't remember him, but he had a lot of questions. I answered them without talking to you. I can't believe I didn't think about how you might feel. It's my bad. I feel just awful."

"I do have memories of him," Esther said. "What did you tell him?"

"I told him you were brilliant, loved books, and that you had great friends. I told him all about you and Sophie. I regret it now, but later, I sent him the picture you saw in Simon's hand."

Esther's head snapped up, and she stood up, opened her mouth, and then not knowing what to say, fell back down onto the couch.

"Wait," Sophie said. "You sent him the exact picture in Simon's hand?"

Grace held both of her hands out, as if she was pleading. "Not the exact one. I sent him a kind of bedraggled copy I took out of the frame when we got this year's picture. The picture Simon had was a copy of that photo. We don't know if it was the same exact photo. But it could be. I am kicking myself. What if it was the same picture? I really believed your dad was working on turning his life around. Like he had finally hit bottom, had an a-ha moment, and maybe someday you could at least be friends."

"Friends?" Esther said. "Friends?"

"You're repeating yourself," Sophie said.

Esther shot up and started pacing. "Did you read the letters before you gave them to me? Do you read them all?"

"Not all of them." Her mom's eyebrows raised, and she tried to smile. Her face turned bright red. "Sometimes I forget how old you are. I still see you as my little girl, and you're not. You're growing up and I need to let you make your own decisions about who to include and not include in your life."

Her mother's distressed face softened Esther's anger, but not her shock. "Is it really my decision to include or not include you?" She raised one eyebrow and squinted at her mother.

A look of pain flashed across her mother's face, and Esther immediately regretted her words.

"No," Papa J said. "It isn't a choice. We love you and we might have to make decisions about who you include and don't include in your life."

"Papa J," her mother said. "I've got this. You're not . . ."

"Not what?" Papa J said.

"Never mind," Her mom said and wiped a tear from the corner of her eye. "Erase, erase. Okay?"

"No," Papa J said.

Her mother's mouth fell open. Esther watched like it was a tennis match.

"I love you and I love the kids that come with you like they are my own. I can't live with them and just watch you all make a mess out of your lives. Esther, we are the adults who love and care about you. We will be heavily involved in every part of your life until you move to a monastery and take a vow of silence. And Grace—I know you love Esther deeply. But you still see her as a little girl. This young lady is brilliant and has a nose for solving mysteries. We need to trust her more and include her more in this conversation. It impacts her." Papa J put his hands on his duty belt and stood tall like a soldier.

"Yes!" Sophie said. Esther's mom turned on Sophie. If Esther's mother's eyes were lasers, Sophie would have been dead.

All the fight went out of Esther. She could tell her mother regretted her choices. "Did you steam open the letters and read them?"

"Very funny. You know I can't boil water or cook anything but chocolate chip cookies," Her mom said. She smiled at Esther who melted the rest of the way and embraced her mother.

Esther texted all the gory details to Parker. Her thumbs flew as fast as her emotions flared. Finally, she told him good night and surfaced from her phone. Sophie was lying on the trundle bed they had moved in for her. She was scrolling on her laptop.

Esther put her phone on the charger for the night. "What are you working on?"

"Didn't you hear me over here calling my computer names and food swearing? You know the photos of the girls in *The End*? They're still up. I am using Google to search for their images on the web. I found one of them in a really strange place. I think we have serious problems."

Esther laid down on her bed, parallel to Sophie's bed and looked at her screen. "Here, let me look closer. The photos are too small."

Sophie turned her laptop and pushed it closer. "Okay, I have the screen split. If you are surfing on this specific search engine, and you see a photo of a face you're curious about, you can right click, and ask this search engine to look for the image on the web. It will pull up similar faces. Sometimes it pulls up so many it's a problem. But in this case, I've found an almost exact match to one of the photos on the event. The only difference is the shirt she's wearing."

"Which one?"

Sophie pointed at one of the photos on social media. "The one of the girl with freckles, brown hair, and hazel eyes like yours. She even has that braid you like to do. A fish something? Anyway, guess where I found her?"

Esther reached out and Sophie handed her the laptop so she could look closer. Her heart sunk. She couldn't breathe. She sat up and kept ping ponging between the pictures. The photo of the girl with the caption, #theend and the picture of the girl on a poster on the National Missing and Exploited Kids website shocked her into silence. She looked at Sophie with her eyes wide and felt her heart beat so fast it hurt.

"She's missing?"

"Worse," Sophie said. "Kidnapped. Her dad was some big politician in eastern Idaho. Her name is Bella Stevens. There are newspaper articles where he claims she was kidnapped, and he is afraid she's dead and says this isn't like her. You know—the usual. But he looks like a nice man, even though he must be desperate. Here, look."

Sophie reached over and opened another tab on the search engine. There was a video of the father weeping during a press conference asking for someone to return his little girl.

Esther was immediately swept back to earlier in the year. They had heard her father had walked away from a prison work program. She was sick, on the couch, when someone knocked on the door. She'd opened the door to a man who looked just like her—her father. But he was almost a full foot taller than she was. Memory after memory flooded her and filled her eyes with tears. Layers of memories revealed themselves. She was small when he stabbed her mother. Running away with her mother, Grandma Mable, and Nephi to hide in Oregon. Secrets she kept and lies she told to friends and neighbors. Her face looking back at her from her father and worst nightmare at their front door asking her to go with him. He tried to take her away. Esther's mother pushed her aside and chased him like a wild mother bear . . .

Lost in memories, Esther's hand's shook as she pressed pause.

"Esther?" Sophie said.

"This is awful. It breaks my heart," Esther said. She wiped a tear from her cheek.

"All I could think about was how close we came to having that be you when your dad tried to kidnap you. I would have gone nuclear and hunted you and your dad down." Sophie took a deep and shaky breath and blew it out.

She held out her hand to Esther. "Here. Let me keep searching for the other girl."

Esther passed back the laptop. "I don't understand. What would a missing girl in Idaho have to do with an event on the Oregon Coast?" Esther opened her closet and took her night hoodie and sweats off their hook.

"I don't understand either. But I am going to blow up the photos I took of the stage and see if any of these girls were in the photos Simon had when he died.

"What do you think that would mean?" Esther pulled off her clothes and changed into the warm sweats she slept in.

"I am trying to put it together but I'm not sure yet."

Esther froze, her foot in midair and a fluffy sock in her hand, looking far away at something that wasn't in the room. "I know what it means. Whoever posted that photo on the event is either related to her, knew about her because they lived in Idaho and thought it would be creepy fun, or worse, they're the person that abducted her. We could have a kidnapper in our midst who wanted to shut up Simon, because he was on to him." She stood up with her mouth open, one sock on, and one still in her hand. Her mind was reeling.

Sophie sat up. "Crepes. So, you're thinking that Simon confronted someone with the photos, and they killed him to keep him quiet?"

"That's exactly what I was thinking. We could have a kidnapper among us, and we don't know who it is. Maybe that's why someone was in your house. Maybe you're next. I think Nephi is right."

"Shut the front door!"

"And lock it." Esther picked up her phone. We have to warn the others. Do you think we can find the other girls if we search tonight? It's almost midnight."

"Piece of cake, piece of pie," Sophie said.

"It's easy?" Esther asked.

"No. That's what I want to eat while we search. Let's go raid the kitchen."

Chapter Fourteen

Fake Followers

Nephi stood so close to Esther and Sophie as they walked across the west parking lot, Esther could feel his breath on her neck.

"Back off, Sasquatch. You're going to give me a flat." Sophie stopped walking, and he ran into her back, nearly pushing her over.

He caught her and stood her up, like a rag doll. "Not on your life. Well, because you have to stay alive."

"We'll be okay," Esther said.

"Not after what you found online. I'm not going to spend the rest of my life eating my cereal with your face on the milk carton." And that was that. Esther knew there was no changing his mind.

"I've been thinking about that," Esther said. "I think Simon found something that got him into trouble. I have an idea. I think we can find out what he knew." She looked behind them to see if anyone was nearby.

"Spill," Sophie said.

"I think we should look inside Simon's house. Maybe there is something in it that will tell us more about what he found. I know that last summer when Papa J got in trouble at work for protecting us, he kept notes in a journal until he was back to work and the chief apologized to him."

"How do you know that?" Nephi said.

"Not telling." Esther smiled sheepishly. "Girls just notice things."

"You're not a normal girl." He chuckled.

"Thanks," Esther said.

"That's not a compliment." Laughing loudly, he gave her a gentle push that almost knocked her off her feet.

"You do make a good bodyguard. You remind me of a rock wall," Sophie said.

"I like that." He flexed his muscles and grinned.

"You're all muscle, alright," Sophie's cheeks turned pink. "Especially between your ears." She looked down and giggled sheepishly.

"Break it up you two." Esther held the library doors opened. Nephi waved and headed toward the gym doors. Sophie followed her into the dark room. Esther was partially blinded after leaving the bright sunlight.

Mephisto was sitting at the table just inside the doors. "Sophie and Esther, can we meet again today?"

"We're really busy, and . . ." Sophie started to explain.

Ms. Priest was nearby, teaching Jax how she wanted the books shelved. "I can let them go with you now. Jax is here." She smiled and patted Jax's arm.

"Great," Mephisto said and stood up.

"Great," Sophie said.

Esther elbowed her and shushed her. "Sophie . . ."

Mephisto opened his office door. "I am so sorry you got sick in my office the other day, Sophie. I hope that doesn't cause this room to be an uncomfortable place for you."

"Not at all, but it still smells a little." Sophie's nose wrinkled.

Mephisto went to his desk and rummaged through his pens. Esther noticed he a small round stone resting by his pencil holder. She remembered Mephisto talking about tossing away her problems by writing them on a stone and throwing them into the ocean. She wondered what word he would put on a stone before he tossed it into the ocean. Maybe, Sophie's name?

He looked up and locked eyes with her. He pulled a legal pad out of his drawer.

"Did you take the garbage out?" Sophie plopped down on the yellow couch.

Esther rolled her eyes at her and when, Mephisto's back was to them as he sipped his coffee, she mouthed *stop*.

"Esther, are you open to sharing what we talked about the other day with Sophie? You know, the day she missed our session?" He sat in the large red chair and facing them.

"I already did. Soph and I talk about everything."

"And, Sophie, what do you think about Esther finally letting go of the toxic relationship she has with her father?" Mephisto raised his eyebrows and tipped his head.

"I feel like it's her decision. Esther and I change, and we've been misjudged before. The only person that can decide what is best for Esther is Esther." Sophie folded her arms and sat back in the yellow couch.

Esther thought about what Sophie said. "I haven't decided one way or the other. The truth is that with everything that's happened, I haven't had time to think about it."

"We often create busyness to avoid hard decisions." He sat forward and look intensely into her eyes. She looked down. The room was silent for a full minute, and then another. Esther recognized the Grandma Mable interrogation tactic and stayed silent. So did Sophie.

Finally, Mephisto broke. "I actually called you both here to check in. It's been a week of toxic stress. Let's all take three deep breaths, shall we?"

Mephisto put his hands open, facing each other at his waist, and sat up straight in his chair. "Join me. Breathe in, one, two, three . . ." He expanded his hands to symbolize full lungs, or at least that's what Esther thought he was doing. "And breathe out, four, five, six. Breathe in, one, two, three . . ." Finally, when Esther was over oxygenated and slightly lightheaded, he stopped.

"Esther, Sophie, Principal Kelly and I met with some of the school board members who have expressed concern about the impact of your recent experiences."

He looked at them for a few seconds. Esther studied his face. She looked down at her hands and realized they were shaking, so she put them in her pockets.

When neither girl spoke, Mephisto sat up, and steepled his hands as he always did, looking down his long nose at them. "Often times, when we are living in a world that feels out of control, as yours must recently, we create a way to take back control. Especially if we have PTSD." He looked directly at Esther. "One might say that you created drama and the myth that Simon was murdered to regain control of your universe . . . make some sense of it. If you can blame someone, then the universe is organized once again."

Esther did like organization. "What if we are sure that he was murdered?"

Mephisto shook his head, making her feel like a little girl in the principal's office. "Esther, Esther, we must learn to trust the universe—trust someone. I was hoping you would trust me."

"We do like organization and trust is an issue for Esther, but we usually trust people we have known longer than a few months," Sophie said. She smirked and tipped her head, giving Mephisto a condescending look that matched his own.

He leaned toward her. "I heard about the break-in, Sophie. Sometimes we lash out when we are really afraid. Was anything taken? Are you distressed? Do we need to call mental health for crisis intervention?" Mephisto sat back and raised his brows, pen in hand, poised to take notes.

"I don't need a crisis intervention. But the burglar will when I get my hands on them. No one messes with the people I love without consequences." Sophie sat up straight and stared at Mephisto, eye to eye.

His mouth opened and closed once or twice, while their eyes were locked. Then his narrowed. "Well, be that as it may, we are all concerned about your safety and well-being. I wanted to tell you in a gentler way, but I was asked to inform you that Principal Kelly had to make a mandatory report to child welfare. We believe you're being neglected. We want to know how best to support you."

A chuckle escaped Sophie's lips, "Bring it." She raised her eyebrows. She unfolded her arms and leaned toward him. "Anyone messes with me, my family or Spam, and they suffer the wrath of Sophie."

He looked down and made notes. "Are you threatening violence?"

Silent again, Esther looked at Sophie out of the corner of her eye. Sophie looked resolute. Mephisto kept writing.

Esther chewed on her lower lip and looked at him through narrowed eyes filling with tears. "We need to get back to the library. Thanks for the help, Mr. Mephisto. I really appreciate."

Finally, Mephisto stopped writing and looked up. "Esther, we still need to discuss how you are doing following your letters from your father."

"Maybe later." Esther looked at Sophie, who was glaring at Mephisto. She stood, and Sophie followed her to the door.

His mouth fell open and the girls silently left his office.

The glass door closed noiselessly behind them, and they remained quiet until they left the counseling offices and rounded the corner to the library.

"Wow, girlfriend. I don't like him. My parents are going to be so mad if they're called by child welfare." Sophie held up her hand to high five Esther. "Don't leave me hanging. Way to power walk out the door and take charge of your life."

Esther was deflated, and her arms hung by her side. "I know. I don't know who to trust anymore."

"Trust me, E. Trust me." Sophie smiled and knuckle punched her.

After walking to the library, Esther put her hand on the door but didn't open it. She let go and looked Sophie in the eyes. "Well, I know one thing. After the pictures were posted in *The End,* and we found the photos around Simon's body, I knew the event and Simon's death were linked somehow. We must go to *The End*, no matter what. I also think we need to see what's in Simon's house, but we can't do it without breaking the law, so that's a no go."

Sophie's eyes narrowed. "You can't break the law, but I can. We're going over there after school."

"How are we going to shake Nephi, our bodyguard?"

"Leave it to me." Sophie pushed the door open and Jax stood there grinning like he had won the lottery.

"Hello, ladies."

After school, Esther was the first to the library. She was standing in Ms. Priest's door talking when Sophie came in.

Ms. Priest smiled and her beautiful white teeth glistened in contrast with her deep red lipstick. "I am actually getting excited to do yoga at the Stone Circle this Saturday. With the new glass roof, weather isn't an issue, and it's so beautiful. Are you joining us?"

"I think so," Esther said. "That's the plan, anyway. We have an event that night, but nothing going on during the daytime."

"Esther." Sophie poked her head into the office. "Are you ready?"

"Sure. Where's Nephi?" Esther followed her out of the library and onto the sidewalk.

Sophie walked towards Simon's cottage. "I told him your grandma was picking us up so we could go to the store."

"You lied?" Esther's mouth fell open. "Sophie, you know I can't do that. I hate lying."

"I know, so I did it for you. Besides, what's the harm? A little white lie won't hurt us." Sophie winked.

Esther's stomach churned, and she felt her face get warm, like she was running. "It really stresses me out. And not just because of my history. It's wrong, you know?"

Sophie shook her head and rolled her eyes. "Is this more stuff from the pastor at the stone church?"

"No. Yes. Well, you know. Yes and no. Grandma Mable always says that all you have in the world is your integrity and that if your word means nothing, you have nothing."

Sophie was silent for a moment, thinking. Then she pushed her glasses up and said, "That's a lot to think about. I'm not sure that's all I have. Let's think about it after we go to Simon's."

Since Simon's house was built on what was originally school property, they didn't have far to go. They turned the corner and Esther noticed Simon's usually pristine yard was looking neglected. Grass was growing in all of the flowerbeds, and weeds were finding a new home in his stone pathway. "Look at his garden. That's a shame."

"Let's go around back," Sophie said.

"Wait. How is this really going to help prove it wasn't an accident?" Esther asked.

"What if he had all those photos he printed from the event and confronted someone with them?" Sophie tried to open the gate to his small backyard. It was locked. She jumped once, then twice to see over the fence.

"What are you doing?" Esther giggled.

Deflated, Sophie shook her head. "Wishing I was taller. I'm trying to see how the gate is locked."

Esther stood on her toes and, holding onto the wood, peeked over the top. "There is a padlock through the handle keeping it from opening on this side." Esther heard men talking and turned around to see Mephisto and Principal Kelly as they rounded the corner. They stopped and stared at the girls.

"Did they see me look over the gate?" Esther asked. She felt like the proverbial deer in the headlights, frozen, not knowing which way to go.

"Yup. They saw it all." Sophie's mouth was open.

"Should we run?" Esther's inner deer suddenly wanted to run.

"Act casual," Sophie said.

Esther's head snapped around as she looked at Sophie with rounded eyes.

Sophie raised her hand and waved. "Hi Principal Kelly, Mr. Mephisto!" She smiled like running into them was the best thing that had happened to her since toaster tarts.

Principal Kelly had on sunglasses masking his eyes, but his frown was visible. He was still in his suit, with his hands in his pants pockets. He looked at Mephisto, who shrugged and smiled. Mephisto didn't seem fazed or even curious. He looked at Esther and shook his head.

"Esther and Sophie, why are you here?" Principal Kelly asked.

"We came to see how Simon's yard was doing," Sophie said. "He loved his flowers."

Esther tried to keep a straight face, amazed at Sophie's audacious lie.

Mephisto smiled from ear to ear. "That is wonderful. I'll get the garbage can out of the back yard for you. They are trying to find a relative to take care of his estate. I'm sure they will appreciate it as Simon would have."

I am going to have to weed now? Esther thought.

Sophie's brows shot up for a micro-second. "Umm, thank you?"

Mephisto beamed. "I can take it from here." Principal Kelly gave Mr. Mephisto the key to the house. "When I find a large photo or a few small ones, I'll send you a picture of what I remove. It will make the posters for the fundraiser for Simon's scholarship more powerful."

Principal Kelly nodded in agreement. "I appreciate your willingness to spearhead the fundraiser."

"I lived here for a few weeks until I found my own place. Simon was a gracious host."

"Yes, he was," Principal Kelly said. "Now, you girls. I appreciate your offer of service, but I don't think you should be in the house or yard alone."

"Oh, well. We totally understand. Good-bye." Sophie waved and took a step, but before her foot even landed, Mephisto spoke.

"Wait," he said. "I don't mind staying while the girls work, if that's okay with you. They'll be outside. We aren't on school property. I have some work to do in the house so I can check on them regularly."

"That's a great idea," Principal Kelly said. "I'll leave you to it, then. I have a meeting with Lars London." He shook Mephisto's hand and headed back toward the school parking lot and his car.

"I'll be right back out. You picked a beautiful day for this." Mephisto let himself into the house.

"I told you lying never paid," Esther said and snickered. "Here, let me try it. I think I'll get sick and leave you to weed alone." She tipped her head and wagged her eyebrows. She couldn't keep a straight face.

Sophie groaned and put her hands over her glasses and eyes. "Look at all these weeds! I don't suppose Mephisto will help."

"He doesn't look like the manual labor type. Where do you want to start?" Esther chuckled.

"Laugh it up, E, laugh it up." Sophie started pulling weeds with her bare hands.

The shadows were long, and the sun was already setting by the time Sophie and Esther headed home.

"I can't believe he sat on the porch and watched us weed the entire time!" Sophie said. "He could have helped."

"You know what I think?" Esther said.

Sophie looked at her and waited.

Esther wiped a hair out of her sweaty face and left a streak of brown dirt across her cheek. The sweat stains on her t-shirt smelled surprisingly worse than they looked. "I think God has a sense of humor. I think this was a grand joke." She laughed. "What I don't understand, is why I have to pay the price for your lie."

Sophie laughed so hard she snorted. "Let's cut through the woods and cut a block off our walk."

They crossed the bridge just before Esther's house and took a worn path through the small woods that would lead to her garage.

Esther grabbed Sophie's arm. "Did you hear that?" They stood still and listened to the wind in the trees.

"Not again. I think you're hearing things."

"That's just it. The birds stopped. Then I heard something . . ." Esther saw a flash of color between the thick pine trees. It was dusk, and the woods were getting dark fast. "Over there. I think I saw something."

"There!" Sophie dug what was left of her dirty nails into Esther's arms. Eyes wide, she scanned left and right.

"Boo!" Nephi jumped out from behind a tree with a silly grin on his face.

Sophie screamed so loud, Esther's ears were ringing when she finally stopped. Meanwhile, Esther didn't scream, she jumped, her heart in her throat and closed her eyes and covered her mouth.

"Nephi!" She scraped Sophie off and gave him a soft push. "You scared us to death!"

"Sasquatch! Not cool!" Sophie screamed, waving her tiny fist at him.

His face fell. He folded his arms and frowned at them. "Do you know what's not cool? What's not cool is being lied to."

Pain started deep in Esther's chest and made her head hurt. She closed her eyes for a minute and realized she felt guilty, seriously guilty, and she didn't like it. She glanced at Sophie, who was silent and looking at her dirty hands.

"I'm sorry." Sophie's voice was soft and gravely. She took her dirty hand and wiped her nose. "I never want to feel like this again."

Nephi melted, his folded arms fell to his side, and he reached out and gathered them into a dirty, sweaty hug. Esther stayed there for a full minute, grateful for his size. It was like being four years old and wrapped up in the arms of a father. Even if he wasn't the best father, you felt safe, loved, and forgiven for whatever you had done.

"Come on. Parker's here with Paisley and Bridget. We've been working on the van and your murder board with Mable. That's how I knew you lied when you said Mable was picking you up."

Worse and worse. Parker knows. Esther sighed. "We're a mess."

"And you stink!" Nephi chuckled and began walking to the house.

"How did you know we were here?" Sophie asked.

"About half-an-hour ago when I realized you weren't with Mable, I started driving. Luckily, I didn't have to go far to see you on the river road. I've been following you the entire time. You two aren't very observant for a couple of amateur sleuths." He laughed at his own joke.

"Good grief," Esther said.

They left the woods, and Parker trotted over to meet them. He stopped a foot away. "Whoa." He started laughing.

Esther stood up straight, put her chin out, and pushed an errant curl out of her face. With a completely straight face, she said, "Excuse me." She brushed the dirt off her hands, and she marched past him with Sophie in tow.

Behind her proud form, the boys laughed even louder.

Esther put her wet hair into a bun and put on her favorite sweatpants and hoodie. Sophie took her turn showering while Esther put mascara on, and for good measure, glittering clear lip gloss and her favorite perfume. She wiped the fog off the mirror. *Who are you kidding? He will never get that memory out of his head. He will forever remember that smell and dirt burned into his brain. He knows she lied!*

Sophie dried off and wrapped herself in a towel. She ran for Esther's bedroom and a change of clothes. A minute later, she was back to share the sink while Esther brushed her teeth.

"Let's go face the fun." Esther put away her toothpaste.

"How many jokes can they make? Should we bet on it?" Sophie put cream in her long black hair and combed it through.

"Five. I say five."

"Ten."

They took the stairs to the living room. Esther's mother, Grace, met her at the bottom of the stairs.

"Esther?"

"Crepes. It's my fault, Mom James." Sophie held her hand up like she was volunteering for duty.

"What?" Esther's mom said. She ran her fingers through her hair and scratched her head. "What's your fault?"

Esther stepped between them. "Nothing, mom. What did you want?"

Her mother grimaced and continued making a mess of her hair. "I . . ." She bit her lip and stood up taller. "You have another letter from your father and if you don't open it, I will." The words tumbled out rapidly. She raised one eyebrow and waited for a response.

"Mom, I can't think about this right now. Sophie and I have a lot to do. Everyone is waiting for us."

Her mom tipped her head, took a deep breath, and opened the envelope.

"Mom!"

"Esther. He's never written a letter every single day. I have a feeling." Her mom looked down and Esther folded her arms in frustration while her mother's eyes scanned the letter, back and forth, back, and forth. Then her mouth fell open. She ran to get her phone off the kitchen table.

Esther followed her mom. "Mom? What is it?"

Her mother held out the letter and shook it while she held her phone to her ear. "I need to speak to the warden. Yes. This is an emergency that involves an inmate."

Esther read the letter, with Sophie looking on.

Dear Esther,

I understand why you don't trust me or won't talk to me. You don't have to reply to my letter, but I am gravely concerned for your safety. I can't write the reason in a letter. Sometimes our mail is scanned. That is why I am begging you to be careful. Don't go anywhere alone. Please, Esther, have your mother call or call together. Or at least answer my collect calls. I don't know why your mom is refusing them, but this is a matter of life and death. Your mother and I talked a few months ago, but something happened after that. Be careful.

Dad

Her mother sat at the table with the phone to her ear and her eyes closed, totally concentrating. "I understand there are call guidelines. We have a family emergency that is a matter of life and death and involves the safety of a child. Okay . . ." She whispered to them, "They're getting me a supervisor."

Esther felt weak all over. She sat close to her mom at the table. Sophie sat next to her. Esther chewed on her lip like she was taking a math test and realized she was holding her breath.

"Hello? I think the line went dead." She stood up, pushing her chair back. "Oh, good. Music. I'm on hold."

"Do you think he is telling the truth? How can you trust him?"

Her mother studied her face while a violin rendition of a classic song leaked from the phone. "I don't know if I can. But I trust me. When he says whatever he wants to, I'll know if it is the truth or not."

"How?" Esther leaned forward. "Please?"

Her mother put a finger up. "Hello? My ex-husband is an inmate. I am an advocate, and my current husband is a police officer. My ex knows this. He has written my daughter a letter that says she is in danger. We need to talk to him. It's important . . . uh, huh. Okay . . . I don't care if you listen in. We need to get to the bottom of this . . . I know it's against rules, but . . . Thank you."

"Well?" Esther said.

"He's getting your dad. It's later there. He had to get permission. If he isn't in his cell or if he's asleep, we'll have to call back tomorrow."

Esther chewed her nails and Sophie stood completely still while the hold music played again. Her mother put the phone on speaker and ran to get a charge cord from the living room. When she had it plugged in, they waited silently. Minutes felt like hours.

Then the music stopped.

"Hello?" Her mom said to the phone on the table.

"Grace?" Her father's voice shot through her like white hot iron.

"Mo? Morgan? We got your letter. Can you talk?"

"They'll record the call, but I don't care. You come first. I only have a few minutes, so I have to make this fast. I'm sorry."

"Go ahead," her mom said. "We're listening."

Sophie ran out of the room and came back with her backpack.

"After everything that happened out there and my extended sentence, this volunteer pastor who counsels with prisoners asked to meet with me to make sure I was stable. We met for a while. Mostly I talked about how to make peace with Esther. He knows everything about you that I do. After you mailed that picture and I showed it to him, Esther was all he wanted to talk about.

"Then, someone here set me up for a fight. I fought back and ended up in solitary confinement for a week. When I got out, the pastor told the warden I was suicidal, and I was back in solitary taking psych evals from the person assigned to people who are a danger to themselves. I tried to explain that he lied. I knew something stunk. When I was finally out of solitary, he was gone. I didn't think too much about it until I realized Esther's picture was gone and then I was worried he was some kind of weirdo. You know? Are you still there?"

Her mother leaned over the phone. "Go on, Mo. We're just taking notes." Esther realized Sophie had a notebook and pen in her hands, ready for him to say more.

"Well, we didn't just talk about Esther. He said she was the spitting image of his high school sweetheart. All I said was that his braided ponytail matched Esther's."

"What does he look like," Esther said.

"Esther? Is that you?"

"Mo," her mother said. "Keep going. Tell us everything you know and what he looks like and his name."

"That's just it. We aren't allowed to know volunteers last names because we're dangerous. We just had a first name. It was Joseph. He looked average—average height, brown hair, hazel eyes, nothing noteworthy really.

"Anyway, as I was saying. The missing picture made me mad and so I told a few inmates. It's like a small town in here, if you get my drift.

"Pretty soon, two other prisoners came to me. They told me that the reason Joseph left was because one of the inmates attacked him. The inmate's girlfriend disappeared. He said she was a runner and he had shared pictures with Joseph and told him all about her. He said she ran in the nearby mountains, and he was always worried about her safety. She used the same route at the same time every day, you know? That's dangerous.

"When she disappeared, for some reason, the prisoner was sure it was Joseph. Joseph wouldn't see him and so the first chance he got, he tried to kill Joseph. He's in for life anyway, you know?"

"Yes," her mother said. "Go on."

"Prisoners gossip. We didn't have any proof, but everyone was convinced it's him because Roger, the librarian did some research. A girl that looks just like Esther disappeared in Eastern Idaho at the last place he said he lived and went to school. And then we realized that another prisoner's daughter who was reported missing about six months ago also has a braid like Esther's, but is a bit shorter. She went to a party, you know, posted pictures of herself on social media and never came home. Oh, and the runner looks like you too, Esther."

Esther's pulse was racing. She was having a hard time keeping up with him, her mind kept snagging on facts. Brown hair. Long hair. Like the pictures Sophie found of the girls who were missing. They looked like her. She folded in on herself, closed her eyes and hugged her stomach. Water ran down her nose, so she felt her clammy fore-head, and wiped it with her sleeve.

"Grace, I was terrified. Everyone is coming to me tell me all about how all he talked to them about was his divorce and how his wife took him to the cleaners, about the same high school sweetheart with a brown braid, and that he focused on peoples' kids or girlfriends."

"Mo. We need a better description. Anything. Even the names of the missing girls."

"I'll see what I can do, but honestly, Grace, I hope you can spot him a mile away. The only thing I can add, is that I think he is around forty years old. You have a nose for people. Trust your judgement. Who is giving you the creeps that fits that description? Has Esther or Nephi seen anyone that fits? And be careful! Don't go anywhere alone. Maybe you need a . . ."

They heard a muffled man's voice.

"I know, I know. Okay, I gotta go. I'll write soon. I'll send everything I know. Everyone will know what we've said shortly. I just hope he doesn't have outside connections with a mole."

The line went dead.

Esther took deep gulping breaths and looked at Sophie who was frantically writing and then at her mother who stared back at her.

"Do you think he's telling the truth?" Esther asked.

"My gut says yes. And, if he lied, he told a very complicated lie. What do you think?" Her mother reached out and took one of her shaky hands in hers. She realized her mother's hands were as clammy as her forehead. *Is she afraid? My gut says he's telling the truth, but I have been wrong before.*

Esther pulled her knees up and, curled up in a ball, nodded. "I do. But what if we're wrong? What if we tell the police and it isn't true?"

Her mother grimaced. "We have to tell Papa J, and we should probably tell Ironpot too. That's the hard part about life. We are often wrong. You get to be wrong. This is one time it would be great if Mo was wrong."

Esther's body relaxed. "It isn't much of a description. I can think of several people that are average height, have brown hair, and have hazel eyes."

"Your creepy neighbor is a counselor, isn't he?" Sophie said.

Grace sat back in her chair and squinted at Sophie, "Yes, but does he really strike you as a killer?"

"I remind you. Ted Bundy was a nice guy who worked on a hotline with advocates like you, and he was a serial killer."

Esther's mom chuckled. "You're right."

"Doctor Phelps is a music therapist, has a ponytail, and fits the description," Esther said.

Sophie put her notepad down on the table and stopped chewing her pen. "But he isn't a pastor, and he has a son."

Esther nodded. "Yes, but the prisoners weren't allowed to know his last name. Okay, so he talked about an ex-wife. But we don't know if there were children or not. We also don't know an exact age. My dad just said, somewhere around forty. We need to write Dad for more details and keep our eyes peeled. I'm not even sure how old Doctor Phelps is. He has one of those timeless faces." She finally unfolded herself and went to the sink to get a glass of water. Her hands shook while she drank.

"Chocolate anyone?" Her mother smiled. "It's recommended in a crisis."

Sophie smiled. "You have chocolate? Where is it? We looked everywhere."

"I should make you close your eyes. You know how I always ask you two to clean and you're always too busy?" Her mom walked to the back porch and opened a small closet full of cleaning supplies. She brought out a bucket and poured Hershey kisses on the table.

Sophie picked one up and smelled it. "You didn't soak these in cleaning fluid, did you?"

"It's a brand-new bucket, pinky promise."

Esther's stomach didn't want chocolate, so she put a few pieces in her pocket. "Everyone is waiting for us downstairs. I guess I should fill them in."

"I'll walk you down," her mother said. They went out the back door and down the gravel path.

"I don't understand, Mom. What would *The End* have to do with Simon?"

"I'm not sure, but my guess is that since he had all the photos you said were posted on the event, he must have known something. Maybe he discovered something and confronted the killer."

"Then, you believe us? It wasn't an accident," Sophie said.

"I've been thinking about it. I know you girls. You're usually right, even if you go about it all wrong. I don't know why I didn't take your word for it in the first place. The only reason I could come up with was exhaustion. It's been a wild year and I just couldn't believe this many things could happen in Necanicum. It's been a year for drama, and I'm drained."

"Queen of D-Nile." Sophie laughed.

"Grace? Is everything okay?" Papa J stood at the door with a soda in his hand, looking confused.

Esther's mom smiled. "So far. Why do you ask?"

"Because you're eating chocolate." Then Papa J grinned, and his eyes twinkled. "Does this mean the diet is over?"

"It isn't a diet. It's a lifestyle," her mom said.

"That's what I keep telling him," Mable said. "Come on, Mary. Time for bed. We can't sand it anymore." She threw her head back and laughed loudly at her own joke. "Say good night."

"Good night, everybody. Miss me!" Mary headed up the gravel path with Mable on her heels.

"Esther!" Parker called from the back of the garage. That's when she realized Parker's father was in the garage. "Guess what! You're never going to guess."

Esther was so overloaded she just smiled back.

"Dad got us all invited to a box and a party at the Seattle Seahawks versus the Green Bay Packers game on Saturday! A friend of his is giving us tickets."

"All of us?" Esther asked.

Parker's face fell. He held his hands up in front of him. "No, I'm sorry. I didn't mean all of us. Just the guys. You know, a guys' weekend. You don't mind, do you? It's this Saturday. We're going up Friday night, doing Pike Place Market in the morning. Then going to the game and coming back Sunday at noon."

Esther forced a smile. "It sounds amazing. I'm glad you're going."

"Wait, there's more," Paisley said. "Because they're going, the moms planned a moms' night out on Saturday. That leaves all of us alone at my house with pizza and junk food Saturday night." She beamed and clapped her hands.

"We have news too," her mother said. "I think you all should hear it."

"Wait, Mom," Esther said. "We can talk later. I want to hear more about what box seats are. I don't get it."

Her mom smiled sadly and gave her a quick hug. "I'll be in the kitchen eating ice cream if you need me." She left by the gravel path.

"Esther, are you serious? You haven't been to a pro-football game?" Parker sounded shocked. "Or soccer? Anything."

Esther looked at her shoes and shrugged, smiling. "Nope. Not one. I haven't even watched one on television without reading a book at the same time or sleeping."

"Dad, we have to take Esther sometime." He turned to Esther, his eyes twinkling. "Let me tell you all about box seats!"

After an hour, Parker seemed calmer as they began cleaning up the garage.

Parker's father ran his hand along the finely primed and sanded body of the van. "I can't believe how hard you've worked on the van. When I saw this hunk of metal, I couldn't imagine it going together and ever running. You had a vision of what it could be."

"It's a classic. When we're done, we could sell it for enough money to pay for college and a new car," Parker said.

His father cleared his throat and looked inside the side door. "I see."

"Seriously. Let me show you an online add for one of these classics."

Mr. Stuart walked over to Parker and hugged him. "I'm proud of you. Money isn't everything."

Sophie leaned close to Esther and whispered, "Says the man who has all the money."

The corner of Esther's mouth turned up.

"Well, I must be off. Early day in the clinic and we need to pack for the trip. Don't forget to pack a warm parka, Nephi." Mr. Stuart zipped up his coat.

"A what?" Nephi's left eyebrow rose, and he shrugged.

Mr. Stuart chuckled. "A warm jacket. We will keep them in the boot in case we need them."

"The boot?" Nephi's voice raised and now both eyebrows were up.

Paisley laughed. "Silly American."

Papa J laughed and clapped Mr. Stuart on the shoulder. "It's going to be a long drive. I can't wait."

They walked outside together. Esther's mom followed them on the path around to the front of the house.

Mable came back into the garage. "Okay, let's get this cleaned up. I can hear every word in my apartment, and I need my beauty sleep for the morning run with your mother, Parker."

"Grandma? I need to tell you all something. I'm sure Mom is telling Papa J."

They gathered around the murder board automatically, sitting on lawn chairs, coolers, and crates. Esther and Sophie told them everything they had learned from her father.

When they were finished, Esther sat next to Sophie on a large cooler. "What do you think?"

"We need a bigger board," Nephi said. "He described half the men in town."

"They don't all have ponytails," Bridget said.

Paisley shook her head. "Hair can be cut. Haven't you heard of Ted Bundy? He looked different in every photo they took of him."

"She's right," Grandma Mable said. "Do you believe him?" She looked at Esther.

There it is, the million-dollar question. "If you mean, do I trust him? I don't know. But what I do know is what Mom said. It's a very complicated story for a lie. And the piece about Eastern Idaho meshes with the photo of the girl Sophie and I identified."

"What girl?" Grandma Mable asked.

Sophie got out her phone and handed it to Mable, who pulled her glasses up to get a better look at the girl's photo. "*The End*? The event at the Stone Circle Saturday?" Sophie said. "Someone posted my school photo, all of our school photos, and a bunch of other kids. We found a few we didn't recognize. I used an online search engine to identify her."

"Huh?" Mable cackled. "You're all so smart. What did you find?"

"Her name is Bella Stevens. She is on the National Missing and Exploited Kids website. There is a video of her dad online too. A newsreel where he is pleading for her to come home."

"It's awful," Esther said. "It broke my heart."

"Anything that involves kids getting hurt is awful. No one can understand it, because it is just plain wrong." Mable handed Sophie back her phone. "It sounds like we need to make a list of men who fit the description Mo gave you."

Sophie walked to the wall. Esther was grateful. She was exhausted. Parker moved to the cooler and put his arm around her. She put her head on his shoulder and felt safer than she had in days.

"Okay. Let's mark everyone who could possibly be this person, until we figure out more about him." She opened the marker.

Paisley pointed at the wall. "Doctor Phelps and Jax, but they aren't murderers. I'm sure."

"How do you know?" Sophie asked.

Paisley pursed her lips and looked at Sophie. "I don't, I guess."

Sophie put a check mark by the new neighbor. "And he is a counselor, so double check."

"What about Bob?" Bridget said.

Sophie checked his name. "Lars London fits the description." She checked his name.

Nephi raised his hand like he was in class. "Principal Kelly." Sophie nodded and wrote his name on the side and put a check by it.

"Who are we missing?" Parker asked.

"Ironpot," Bridget said.

"He didn't do it," Esther snickered.

Bridget nodded. "You and I know he didn't, but he also fits the description. Do you see what I mean? We need more information. At least an identifying mark like a tattoo."

"I'm tired," Esther said.

"I bet you are," Mable said. "We can work on it more in the morning."

"No. Keep going." Esther snuggled in closer to Parker. "We have to do this. *The End* is coming."

Sophie wrote Mephisto and checked it. "How many of these names have motives?"

"Lars London," Esther said. Her voice betrayed her need for sleep. "He wants to destroy our beloved library. In fact, he wants to tear down the whole school and put in a parking lot." She giggled.

Sophie chuckled, "You're so tired, you're getting slap happy. We'd better pick up the pace."

"Bob's motive is lame," Nephi said. "It doesn't make sense. Unless he's getting a kickback from London. They both showed up around the same time."

"What if the motive is just plain cracked? Like my stalker? He just fixated on me and kidnapped me and took me up the mountain to kill me?" Paisley said. "He only had one motive, complete selfishness and, well, he needed help."

Sophie nodded in agreement. "What are motives for serial killers?"

"Oh, I know that one. I help Mom research for her books." Bridget put her hand out and Sophie gave her the marker. "One reason is they are addicted to taking a life. Some of them want revenge and they either got it and it didn't feel the way they expected, or they haven't gotten it. They are practicing. And the last reason is just gross. They're usually men." She shivered and handed the marker back to Sophie.

Grandma Mable cleared her throat. She shifted in her lawn chair. "I know you want to know who it is, Esther. I loved Simon, and I understand the need for justice. If your dad is right, we have to resolve this." She leaned forward in her seat. "But this time, it feels like the only way to catch this shark is to swim with it and that is a lose, lose situation." Frowning, she sat back, folded her arms, and stared at the wall. A look crossed her face, like someone who just remembered a word they had lost. She sat forward again. "Who on the list had past involvement with Simon?"

Sophie stepped back from the wall. "We know he and London were arguing about selling a house, which is really a fight about money. Money is a solid motive. Especially if London needs the school grounds to make a large amount or if London is in debt. I'll check it out online."

"Mephisto stayed in his house and roomed with him," Esther said. "But I think he's a stretch. He told me he worked at a college campus and before that he worked at another high school. I don't know. I think he is trying to help me, and I appreciate it. Plus, even though he's a counselor, he has things like crystals in his office. He doesn't strike me as a pastor."

Sophie smiled and shrugged. "I don't like him."

"He did make you sick." Nephi laughed at his own joke.

Esther sat up. "Mephisto was the first person to help us when Simon died. He ran hard enough to get to us. He was sweaty. I think he was trying to protect us from the chaos when he sent us to his office to wait for the police."

"I don't think a killer would take a jog right after committing the crime. He would have had to go out the back, down the tunnel, and come around from the gym to the lobby doors." Paisley said. "I mean, why would he kill him and then show up at the other doors? What brought him there?"

Esther's mouth fell open. "You're right . . . how did he know we were there?"

"I screamed like a little girl," Sophie said.

Nephi gave her a friendly push and smiled. "You are a little girl."

Sophie's cheeks turned pink, and she turned her nose up at Nephi. "I screamed, okay? Esther did too. It wasn't a long scream. I mean, what would you do if you found a body of someone you liked laying like that?"

"Of course, you screamed," Bridget said.

Something tickled Esther's memory, like seeing an old friend and not remembering their name. It would drive her crazy until she remembered it. Whatever was lost in the corners of her mind flitted away.

"Yes, but could he hear it in the hall? Why was he there? Class was in." Paisley sat forward and narrowed her eyes.

"That's easy to solve," Mable said. "All you have to do is go back to school and scream, while someone waits outside the doors to see if you can hear it."

Paisley looked at Esther. "Let's try it tomorrow after school, before rehearsal."

"I'm in," Esther said.

Nephi yawned. "I think you should take Bob off the list. He didn't have any involvement besides working under Simon, and I can't believe a job as a janitor is a motive."

Paisley yawned, and then gave Nephi a gentle push. "Don't yawn. It's contagious. He's right. Phelps and Jax don't have a dog in the fight either. The play was happening one way or the other. I don't see any connection to Simon."

"I agree with Paisley." Bridget yawned while she talked and stretched. "Mom is paying Mr. Phelps a lot to tutor me individually. He is getting the pathetic district salary and a monthly consulting fee for working with Mom. It's like getting paid twice for the same job. The end of the play is the end of double dipping, unless they hire him full time. And he rented rooms from your neighbor, Marion. Jax said the rooms are gorgeous and cheap." Her eyes were bloodshot, and her lids drooped.

"Well, that makes the creepy neighbor who is a counselor interesting." Sophie tapped the marker on her open palm. "Would taking Phelps off mean that Jax is off the board too? I don't think Phelps worked at the prison. Didn't he say they were in Seattle before they moved here? That accounts for his time if it's true and means he wasn't volunteering at a Utah Prison. I'll try to verify it online. If he's a pastor, he should be licensed somewhere."

Esther stood up. "Paisley, I keep thinking about what you said. I swear you're a genius. Let's look at timelines." She opened her hand and Sophie put the marker in it. "Principal Kelly has been here. If it was Principal Kelly, wouldn't he have killed Simon earlier? Although Phelps is a music therapist, so something like a counselor, Phelps is clearly interested in your mom, Bridget—but don't say I said so. He strikes me as someone who likes quality people, not a serial killer fixated on kids. And as much as I hate to admit it, Jax is alright."

"What?" Sophie asked. "Back up. Madison and Phelps?"

Paisley looked at Bridget, who rolled her eyes and shrugged. "I wasn't supposed to tell anyone that my mom and Doctor Phelps went out on a date. I am sure we can cross him off because his timeline doesn't fit with your dad's story. His resume said he was in Seattle before he started with working with Mom."

"Resumes lie. I'm putting him on the list of things I need to validate. I think you're right, it's easier to work by process of elimination," Sophie said. "Let's also look at alibis for the day of the murder. For example, we know where Bob was, but he was cleaning alone until Madison showed up. Did she ever say what took her to the auditorium?"

Esther closed her eyes and thought back. "She told us at the Stone Church she was with Bob and looking for Simon, so she would check out the auditorium. That's if I remember correctly."

Mable crossed her legs and tilted her head. Her full attention was on the wall. "Let's recap. Simon was murdered, but the police are sure it's an accident. We think whoever did it organized *The End* or is associated with the event because of the photos, but we don't have any proof. The photos are missing, and they've closed the case. Sophie doesn't want to show them the video and picture you took, because that could land you two in trouble with the police.

"We have a few suspects, but only one with any real solid motive, Lars London. We may or may not have a serial killer who has stolen a photo of Esther and may or may not have been in town. Principal Kelly is annoying and a creep but seems more interested in Ms. Priest and was here when the pastor was in Utah. Doctor Phelps, and Bob are unlikely suspects because they lack a motive and are nice. And a few hundred other locals fit the description of the potential serial killer, which makes it almost impossible to locate the killer based on your dad's description. The good news is, we have a description of a possible suspect that narrows it down a bit. For example, we know it isn't a woman if Mo is right." Grandma Mable looked at Esther who smiled and nodded in agreement. "That's half the population checked off the list."

The whole room was silent while they digested her discouraging words.

A smile spread across Mable's face. "It reminds me of my past and working as an investigator with my husband, the official M.P. It's impossible to solve and yet, you're well on your way."

"Are you kidding? You just burst any bubble of hope I had left," Sophie said.

Mable cackled. "You're a smart girl, Sophie. But in this case, you're wrong to lose hope. You have all the pieces. You just don't know how to put them together."

Parker squeezed Esther's shoulder and gave her a half smile. "All I know is Esther and the rest of us need to get some sleep, we'll be smarter in the morning."

"Or not," Sophie said.

Esther and Parker were the last people in the garage. They stood side by side in front of the van, arms folded, admiring their work.

"It's perfect," Esther said.

Parker put his arm around her. "I can't believe what a good job Paisley did on the interior. I knew she loved to sew, but this is a work of art."

He looked down at her and gave her a sweet kiss.

"I better get to bed. Mom would kill me if she knew I was outside alone, kissing a boy." She studied his serious eyes and smiled.

"A boy?" Any hint of happiness vanished from his face. "I'm just a boy?"

"No. Well . . . yes?" Esther said.

He stepped back and looked down at his feet. There was a solitary screw laying on the ground. A tire popper. He kicked it with his toe for a minute.

"Parker? What's wrong?"

He took a deep breath, looked up, and smiled, but his eyes looked sad. "Can I admit something?"

"Always."

"Sometimes I get insecure. I watched you with Jax in the library and for the first time, I wondered if we would always date or if someday you would go away."

She felt like he had punched her in her gut. "I'm not going to change. Sophie and I can't even get into the colleges we want unless we do something amazing." She tried to joke, but it fell flat.

He nodded but didn't look at her. "I'm going to be going away to school. Jax will be here. Things happen. Maybe you'll change."

"People don't really change."

"Not even for the better?" He tilted his head and grimaced. "I know you have a lot of history with your dad. But I disagree. Sometimes people change."

Now it was her turn to frown. She folded her arms. "He won't."

Parker raised his eyebrows and chewed on his lip. "I know I shouldn't be jealous of Jax. I have to go. We're going to drop the van in Portland on the trip to Seattle. My dad found an auto painter he likes. He's going to pay him to paint it for me."

"That's great." Esther spoke quietly, still shaken by the idea that he didn't really trust her to be there for him. She didn't know what to say. *Reach out, hug him, tell him you'll never leave him. Why does he even care? What right does he have to judge me? He has a father who loves him . . . Look at the pain in his eyes!*

It was silent for a minute. "Well, I better get going." He gave her a tight hug, kissed her forehead, picked up the screw, and got in the van. It started right up.

She stepped to the side, and he drove away, leaving her alone in an empty garage.

"Esther?" Sophie whispered.

"Hmm?"

"Are you awake?"

"No." Esther rolled over to look at Sophie on the trundle bed. The curtains were opened, the moon was full, and light spilled across Sophie's bed. She pulled Ms. Molly closer and laughed softly. "I'm awake now."

Sophie lay on her back, her arms folded over the blankets. "Are you afraid? I mean, what if it's a serial killer?"

"I wish I wasn't."

"Me too. I'd much rather be mad. How could someone hurt a nice girl like that?" Sophie said.

"We don't know that they did. That's the hard part. It's just all pieces of a puzzle without the edges."

"We have to go to the event." She rolled on her side so she could see Esther. "I'm afraid if we don't, it will always be hanging over our heads. We need to try to talk to your dad again. We need a better description, an age, something."

"I'll write to him tomorrow."

"I wish we could call or knew an email. Something." Sophie rolled back onto her back. Her sheets rustled as she adjusted her blanket. "You know, my dad always says people don't change when he talks about his family. I've never met them."

"Really? I didn't know that. How could I not know that?" Esther said.

"I don't think about it much, except when I think about your dad. Then it's like a tape recording plays in my head." Sophie lowered her voice and sounding like her dad said, "People don't change."

"I've changed," Esther said.

"Me too."

Esther stroked Miss Molly and snickered. "I hope people can change. If not, Mrs. Stuart is in for a rude awakening and all of our moms are going to go back to donuts, coffee, and pizza on Friday nights."

"Then I think I'll pray that people don't change. I would love that."

"Funny, isn't it? The one person I have tried to avoid, the person that has hurt me the most, is the person we need to talk to. The one person I have been terrified of, is trying to help," Esther said.

Sophie looked at Esther in the moonlight. "It would be funny if he hadn't given a serial killer your picture."

"Did you see where Nephi is sleeping tonight?"

"No."

"I caught him when I got up to get a drink of water. He's sleeping on the floor with Spam in front of the bedroom door."

"Then we're safe," Sophie said and rolled over, her breathing becoming steady in the quiet night.

Chapter Fifteen

Invited, Maybe, Going

"Okay, people. Do you all know what you're doing?" Paisley said. She stood on the first step of the stage, and they filled the auditorium seats. "Let me recap, and then we'll meet here again for auditions next week. I will send you a calendar invite to every night or rehearsal you're required to attend or support. Check your email! Esther and Jax have their scripts as does Parker, who plays Jax's rival for the princess's attention. Bridget, plan a run-through of your number at our first rehearsal. Madison, you will invite a musician to play some numbers before the play, to beef up the night. I will work with the boosters to supply refreshments and charge an arm and a leg for tickets. We are going to raise money for the Simon Scholarship Fund. And Madison and I will prepare a poster in his memory to remind people to donate. Bob! Wake up, Bob. Meet me here tomorrow morning. Sophie, you too. We need to talk props. That's a wrap, people. You know what to do!"

Parker stood up. "I'll be right back." He was trotting up the auditorium aisle before Esther could say goodbye.

Nephi leaned closer to Esther and Sophie. "She's magnificent."

"Stop drooling. She's going to have to be our bodyguard since you're leaving for Seattle tonight."

He smiled. "You're eating pizza and ice cream."

"Yes, I am," Sophie grinned.

Esther zipped her hoodie and picked up her backpack. "Man. You were right, Soph. Paisley is one amazing organizer. Come on, let's go."

"Didn't you have to test your scream tonight?" Nephi said. "You know? To see if you could hear it outside the auditorium?"

"Done and done," Sophie said. "We did it before the meeting. You can definitely hear me scream outside the auditorium."

Parker came trotting back down the aisle with a massive smile on his face. He passed Esther and gave Nephi a buddy smack on the back. "Dad and Papa J are here. Everything is in the truck. Let's go. We want to get to Seattle in time for dinner on the pier."

"Good-bye," Esther said.

Parker swung around, hugged her hard and fast. "Miss me. And don't let Jax take any of your time and attention. I'm going to make Paisley cancel the kiss in the play."

He didn't wait for a response. Parker and Nephi trotted up through the doors chatting and laughing. The doors closed and the world suddenly felt empty and lonely. Esther sighed.

"Come on, E. Let's go home and pack for Paisley's." Sophie adjusted her backpack and walked ahead of her out of the auditorium.

Paisley, Jax, and Bridget were on the stage talking to Bob, who was showing them his paint supplies. They passed Madison, whose eyes sparkled while she talked quietly with Doctor Phelps. Ms. Priest was long gone. The halls were dark in the early evening hours, and so was the library.

Esther pushed the doors opened. The cool evening salt air blowing in felt good on her face. The night was dark with clouds. The light of a single streetlamp in the fog marked the distance to the street.

"Crepes and graham crackers. Nephi was our ride," Sophie said.

Nephi's truck was parked under the single streetlamp, abandoned for a weekend of fun. "We have got to take the test for our permits so we can get a driver's license."

"It's too late now."

"Should I call Grandma or Mom for a ride?"

"No. I heard Madison saying she was late for Zumba. We can walk." Sophie made the decision for them both. "And while we're at it, let's walk by Simon's house."

"There's no way to avoid it." Esther started down the stone steps. "This place really needs gargoyles. Maybe if we ask, Madison will buy them."

Sophie laughed softly. "It's creepy out tonight."

"It's just fog."

They left the parking lot, passed the south end of the stone school. The lights were on in Simon's house. Both girls stopped and stared. They looked at each other and silently agreed. They walked closer.

Esther turned and tried to take the edge of the yard and stand deep in the shadow of a small tree.

The inside of the house was lit up by two lamps. It was a small house. The living room looked tidy, like Simon. The kitchen was granite, stainless steel, and grey walls. The light was on a single desk. A computer monitor was on. A man sat with his back to them, looking at the screen.

Noiselessly, they crept closer.

Esther tapped Sophie, leaned into her ear, and whispered. "Can you tell who that is?"

Sophie shook her head. She opened her cell phone and took a single photo. The flash was bright in the dark night. It blinded Esther.

"Sophie," she hissed. "Run."

Sophie passed her and then looking over her shoulder, ducked into the dark woods. Esther didn't bother to look back. She knew whoever it was, was dressed in all black and didn't want their photo taken. The two girls barreled through the silent woods—alerting every bird, owl, or animal for hundreds of yards around them.

A few minutes later, they came out of the woods and slammed into the garage door. Esther spun around and looked wildly in every direction. Then she and Sophie took the trail on a dead run. The front door was locked. Her hands shook as she fished for the key under the flowerpot. Spam barked viciously on the other side of the door.

"I hate locking the house," Esther whispered. She fumbled with cold fingers until she opened the front door. When it opened, she tossed the key under the pot. They went in and slammed the door, locking it, and leaned against it, huffing and puffing. Spam licked Sophie's face, and his little body trembled with joy.

"You left the key out there?" Sophie said.

"Crepes." Esther stood on her toes and peered out of a tiny window in the doors. She opened the door a tiny bit and peeked out. As fast as she could she knocked the planter over and took the key, locking the door again. "Everyone must still all be at the stone church."

They slid down the door and sat on the floor. Listening intently to every noise, or sound. Spam panted in the dark.

"Who was that?" Esther asked.

"I couldn't tell. They had on a black stocking hat." Sophie fished her phone out of her pocket. She hugged Spam and enlarged the blurry photo she had taken.

Esther turned on every light on the first floor of the house and pulled the front room curtains closed. Sophie put Spam in his basket by the fireplace. On the kitchen side of the two-sided fireplace, Esther put diet cokes on the table.

Sophie looked at the photo on her phone.

"Can you see anything?"

"I can't tell who it is." She handed Esther the phone. "But if you zoom in, you can see what they are looking at."

Esther squinted, and the tiny photo came into focus. Her head snapped up, and she locked eyes with Sophie. "It's *The End* page on social media on the computer monitor."

Handing Sophie her phone, she pulled out her own and opened social media. New photos were on the event. They seemed personal. "I think they are sending a message." Fear turned to anger as the slow burn of fury rose from deep inside her gut.

The first photo was of Mary again, in the Stone Church, opening the door. The next was of Bridget sitting on stage in the new park, playing her guitar. The last new photo was of the Stone Circle with a storm raging behind it. The caption read, "See you tomorrow!" Almost every student in town had commented. Things like, "Can't wait" and "Bring it!"

"At least we know for sure that whoever is doing this is linked with Simon and I am sure they must be the killer," Esther said. "Who else would dress like that and make every hair on my arms stand on end?"

"Right? Did you write to your dad?"

"I did, but letters take three days to get there from here. There's no such thing as overnight to Necanicum. By the time we hear from him . . ."

The old-fashioned house phone began ringing in the living room. Both girls stood up.

"No. It can't be," Esther said. "Too much of a coincidence." They stood frozen for another ring, then scrambled to the phone.

"It's probably your auto warranty," Sophie said. "I hate those calls."

Esther scooped up the old black receiver and listened. "This is a collect call from the Point of the Mountain Correctional Facility. Will you accept this call? If so press one."

Esther hit one.

"Grace?" It was her father's voice. Her heart raced. She never thought she would be happy to hear him talk.

"Dad?"

"Esther is that you?"

"Yes, Dad! Dad, I think the killer is here. I need to know what he looks like."

"What's going on?"

"It's important! Okay?" Esther motioned for Sophie to bring her school backpack to her. She fished in it for a pen or pencil.

"He's got brown hair, hazel eyes, medium height, medium build," her dad said.

"I know that. But how old is he? How does his skin look?"

"I don't know for sure, but he looked like he was in his late thirties, maybe forties."

"Did he have any tattoos or scars?" It was quiet on the line. Esther rubbed her head.

"Not that I know of. I can ask around." The line was quiet for a moment. "I guess what I noticed most was his braid. It isn't unusual for men to have braids or even makeup. But the braid was like the one you wore. I don't know what it's called, but it looks like a zipper. Oh, and he had a small silver earing in his left ear."

Esther closed her eyes and gritted her teeth. "That helps, but he can change his hair and take out an earring. How can I find him, if I don't have any identifiable characteristics?"

"There can't be that many men with long hair or braids in a small town like yours."

"Oregon? You obviously haven't met River Peace who owns the radio station or a hundred other men in town."

Sophie leaned into the phone and said, "Hair can change, even if people can't."

"I hope people and hair change. If they don't, then I have no hope of making amends and being any kind of a father, ever."

"He didn't have a tattoo. Anything?" Esther leaned against the wall, eyes closed, frustrated.

"No, not that I can remember."

Sophie leaned into the phone again. "What about an accent?"

"Esther, what happened? Has something happened?"

"Someone died. They think it was an accident, but we are convinced it wasn't. It seems to be tied to an event." Esther explained using her hands even though he couldn't see her.

"Don't go to the event!"

Esther held the phone away from her face.

"Esther! Esther, don't hang up!"

Her heart jumped at the shout on the other end of the line. "You're not my father! You can't tell me what to do." She hung up.

"Esther! What did you do?" Sophie picked up the phone and listened to the buzz of the dead landline. Slowly, she hung it up.

"He doesn't have the right to talk to me that way!" Esther stomped her foot.

"He was just afraid you would get hurt! He was our only lead. If there was a clue, he had it." Sophie shook her head in disbelief.

Esther put her fists over her eyes and growled. "I just can't trust him."

"No one is asking you to. I just need to trust you and you need to trust yourself."

They stood silently for a minute. Spam whined.

Esther's arms fell to her side, her clenched fists relaxed. "I am so sorry, Soph. I don't know what came over me."

"I do. A lifetime of grief and fear." Sophie sighed. "It's okay. We don't have a lot to go on. But now we know he isn't old, and he isn't super young. He's somewhere in the middle. He'll write if he thinks of anything else."

The house was silent again.

"Let's find something to eat." Esther walked to the kitchen.

"I miss our bodyguard," Sophie said to Spam.

Chapter Sixteen

Status Update

The sun rose in the east, and gradually found its way to the windows on the south side of Esther's round bedroom. It wasn't strong enough to stir Miss Molly, who had left the bed for the laundry basket in the dark closet.

The sound of the Ode to Joy, Beethoven's Symphony number 9, began when the alarm went off on Esther's phone. She smiled at the sound, stretched, and let the music go on.

"Kill it," Sophie said, and put her pillow over her head.

"Don't you like Ode to Joy? It's six-thirty. We have to get up."

"I love any ode after breakfast," Sophie said. "Hey, where's Spam? I had her under the covers with me so she wouldn't chase Molly."

"We have yoga in the park in thirty minutes. We need to find him." Esther looked under the bed. "Spam?"

"Here, Spam." Sophie made kissing sounds sending Esther into a fit of giggles and an impression of Sophie's kissing sounds.

"Shush. I hear him." Esther opened the bedroom door. She heard scratching and barking coming from Mary's room.

"Sit, Spam. Sit. Why won't you listen to me?" Mary said.

Esther opened Mary's bedroom door. "Mary. How did you get Spam out of my room?"

"I just opened the door and invited him to breakfast." She pointed at a bowl on the floor of something smelly.

"What did you feed him?" Esther recognized the smell as canned cat food but wasn't sure.

"Here you are," Sophie took Spam from her arms and back to the bedroom.

"It's Molly's food. Molly won't mind."

"Never feed a pet without asking an owner. You never know what might make a dog or cat sick. Can I have the can?"

Mary pulled the package from her little pink garbage can.

"Thanks, Mary."

"When do I get a pet of my own?" Mary's lower lip quivered.

Esther's heart melted. She knelt by Mary and scooped her into a tight hug. "Listen, Goober, I'll tell Mom, the next pet should be yours. Okay? We can go to the shelter next week and dream. Would that be nice?"

Mary wiped her nose with her hand and nodded.

Esther and Sophie were both waiting in the SUV when her mother came racing down the stairs. "Where's Mary and Mom?"

"They left already. We were happy to wait," Esther said.

"You mean happy to miss yoga." Her mother stowed her yoga mat in the back.

"I love yoga," Sophie said. "Any time after eight in the morning on a Saturday. No one should get up before the eights on a Saturday."

The sun was brilliant and in rare form for an Oregon morning. The dew defied the light, but it looked as if the sun might win the day. The SUV crossed town using the neighborhood back roads to avoid tourist traffic. With every window open, Grace rounded the Cove and took the road up the mountain. The mountain pushed past the shore and more than a half mile into the ocean which beat upon its rocky beaches with violent waves. Despite years of erosion, the pine tree-covered mountain survived.

The houses along the cliff got bigger and further apart. A tenth of a mile past the last house, the road opened to the trailhead parking lot. Madison had purchased all the undeveloped property on the cliff side of the mountain. It wasn't safe to build houses or condos on, but it was the perfect place for Madison's park that would be her lasting contribution to Necanicum.

Grace parked next to Madison's Range Rover, Mable's small truck, and Melissa Stuart's SUV.

"Hey, check out the new sign for the park. I can't believe we haven't been up here already," Esther said.

Sophie and Esther gathered their things and followed her mother up a gently sloping paved trail. It was consumed by trees and then veered slightly to the right where it opened up to the park and the ocean beyond it.

Sophie dropped her bag and her mouth fell open. "Holy cannoli, it looks so real. I can't believe Madison did this."

An exact replica of the Stonehenge in Britain perched on the northwest cliff's edge, on a carpet of green grass and tiny white daisies. It looked like it had been there a thousand years. Just past the stones, the ground dropped away. All you could see in one direction for miles was rolling ocean. If you looked to the left, you could see a small rock island and its ancient white lighthouse just a few miles out to sea. The mesmerizing waves splashed against the rocks, and sea lion bathed on the tiny shore in the sunlight. You couldn't see Necanicum unless you leaned out. The small town was there, but the way the clearing was made hid any sign of it. It felt secluded and magical.

Just to the south of the stones, the ground sloped down slightly to an odd-shaped cement stage with ramps on both sides. It was like someone had poured the cement and it was a misshapen puddle. Four grey cement statues of tree trunks held a piece of plexiglass over the stage. It was slightly sloped in a way that would protect it from the wind and allow the rain to run off the back.

The stage faced eight circular rows with stone stairs ascending in the center. She walked closer to the seats. Slabs of stone made each seat look like it belonged right where it was laid.

"This is a work of art," Esther said.

"Thank you." Madison startled Esther. She smiled. "It's just how I dreamed it would be. Sadly, the trees absorb the sound, so terrible acoustics, but . . ." She shrugged.

"All of this came out of your head?" Sophie said.

Madison laughed melodically. "Yes. Just like amazing things come from you and your parent's brilliant minds. I believe everyone has a talent. I love planting seeds and watching them grow."

Melissa Stuart turned on earthy, meditation music. Little Mary unrolled her mat near Mrs. Stuart, calm and confident.

Esther leaned down, closer to Sophie and asked softly, "Who is that child and what have they done with Mary?"

Sophie smiled, and they joined the others on the cold cement.

"Do you feel better?" her mother asked.

Esther smiled. She still wasn't ready to talk. The peace of the morning had left her feeling calm, a feeling she realized she hadn't experienced for a while. Her mother gave her a quick hug and held Mary's hand as they followed the other adults to the parking lot.

"Esther," Paisley called her in a soft tone and hung back from the moms. She and Bridget waited until the moms were out of sight.

Paisley flashed a brilliantly white smile. "Our moms have decided to go to the Train Station Restaurant at Douglas Crossing tonight. They will be on the mountain between here and Portland for hours. Then they're going to stay at Madison's and use the hot tub and sauna. Bridget and I talked them into giving us a pizza budget and letting us all stay at my house alone. Will you and Sophie come?"

"*The End* is tonight. We plan on watching the party and hoping the person who organized it shows up. Especially after we saw someone working on the event in Simon's house," Sophie said.

"Don't worry. We're going to make an appearance at the party." Paisley winked.

Esther gasped. "You want to go to *The End*? It could be dangerous. The police won't investigate and I'm sure they aren't invited. We don't even know if it's chaperoned."

Paisley adjusted her yoga bag and mat and gave Bridget a knowing look. "Bridget and I talked. We know you and we know that after everything that's happened nothing is going to keep you from finding out who organized *The End*, and if they killed Simon. We've talked to everyone in school. We even tried to talk them out of going, but no one listened. Everyone is going."

Sophie smiled. "Told you so."

Paisley went on. "Actually, it should be pretty safe. Anyway, it's within walking distance of our house. If we get nervous, we scoot home. Especially if people start drinking. I think I can fix you up so you blend in."

"I agree, if we don't go, we miss our chance to find out who organized the event and if they are the prison pastor my dad called us about. With the threats to me and everything that's happened to Sophie, I don't feel like we have a choice. I just wish Parker and Papa J were coming. It's like being caught between two bad choices," Esther said.

"We don't have to actually attend the party. We could just watch. Being in a crowd feels safer than being alone, but I agree, it's risky," Paisley said. "At dusk, you can hide a whole herd of elk in these trees."

"Seriously? How do you sneak around a party that size? You're talking over two hundred kids." Esther shook her head. "The Stone Circle isn't big enough to get lost in."

"Come on. We can do this. You know this mountain better than any of us. Our house is just down the street. We can walk up and slip into the forest before we even get close," Paisley said.

"I agree with Paisley. But keep our plans on the down low," Bridget said. "My mom's a bit overprotective. I've already had a running lecture about what we can and cannot do tonight. I had to promise to practice for the play, and not watch scary movies."

"Come on, E. We can't prove I was poisoned, but everyone knows someone broke into my house. If I'd have been home, I would have been forced to seriously injure them. I think the killer has to be London, or the creepy neighbor."

Sophie's hands were on her hips. "I think your dad is telling the truth. We have a serial killer in our midst that took that girl from Idaho. I know you don't believe he's changed, but why lie? Your parental units want us to let Detective Kohornen handle Simon's death—Kohornen, the detective that botched Paisley's abduction!"

Esther kicked the dirt, squared her shoulders, and looked at her friends. "I agree totally. Kohornen isn't going to solve this. But we have to play it safe. We aren't going to the party. We are going to fade into the background and watch."

"Deal." Paisley put her hand out, Bridget put her hand over Paisley's, and Sophie put her hand over Bridget's. They all looked at Esther who hesitated. Sophie gave Esther the stink-eye. "E?"

Esther put her hand on top of the pile. They looked at each other and Paisley bounced the pile and said, "One for all."

"Technically there were three musketeers. There are four of us. We should get swords." Sophie pushed her glasses up her nose, grinning.

"I'll bring pizza. Will that work?" Paisley wagged her eyebrows.

"One for pizza! Now, what about Spam?" Sophie asked.

"Cornwallis, our dog, is pretty chill with other dogs. How does Spam do?"

"I don't know. I haven't really taken him anywhere. If Mom hadn't left in such a hurry and I wasn't going to be so close by, we would have used our groomer as a dog sitter."

Paisley smiled. "It's going to be a blast. Bring Spam. What about Molly, your cat, Esther? Is she okay at home alone?"

"Only if I leave her the remote and her favorite snacks."

Chapter Seventeen

Fur-real, Pics Please

Esther held her and Sophie's things while Paisley unlocked the front door to her family's home, the Captain's Cove Mansion. When people fussed about the house, Paisley shrugged and said it was just an old Queen Anne Victorian by the sea.

As soon as they were close to the house, Paisley's gold labradoodle rushed to the door, barking and scratching joyfully. Paisley cracked the door and slipped in to get her dog kisses. A stubby tail wagged the entire dog. "Hello, baby. How's my General Cornwallis? Did you miss me? Did you miss me?"

Cornwallis had to inspect Esther and Bridget. Almost like a cat, he rubbed against their legs until they gave him love, petting and scratching his back and behind his ears.

"Sophie?" Esther said.

Sophie peeked around the door jamb, holding a small crate with Spam shivering inside. Cornwallis almost knocked Sophie's tiny frame over as he barked and then sniffed Spam. "Hello Cornwallis, this is Spam. It's okay, Spam. It's okay." She put down the crate and knelt on the floor letting Cornwallis love on her. She hugged the familiar, happy dog and let him lick her face.

"Cornwallis, Meet Spam." Sophie pushed Cornwallis back gently and took Spam's shivering body out of the crate and sheltered him in her lap. Gradually the dogs checked each other's nether regions out and must have passed the sniff test. Spam jumped down and Cornwallis took him to see his mansion.

The girls followed the dogs into the spacious and cozy library. Paisley turned on lights as they went. They crossed the mahogany room to light the gas log in the carved marble fireplace. A new photo hung over the fireplace. It was a beautiful family photo of the Stuarts in denim and white standing in the surf.

Esther felt a pang of envy looking at Parker's happy family, but quickly reminded herself that she just wanted what they had. A family that didn't expect perfection, forgave easily, and loved deeply. Her family photo, taken at her mother's marriage to Papa J, was a conglomerate of young, old, new, adopted, and absent. Her heart caught fire just thinking about it.

Paisley pulled her phone out of the back pocket of her jeans. "My mom keeps texting. For some reason she doesn't like the fact that we are here, the guys are in Seattle, and they are on the mountain. I think she's having a panic attack." Paisley's laugh was deep and infectious.

"My mom is the same way. Always worrying. It drives me cray cray," Bridget said.

"And we love it when they're gone and we get a little freedom to party." Sophie's smile looked slightly wicked to Esther. Bridget and Paisley laughed with her.

"Do you think the dogs will be okay while we're gone?" Esther asked.

Paisley nodded.

"I'll leave Spam's crate in the corner so he can take a break from his new friend if he needs to." Sophie put Spam's water and food bowls in the kitchen. "Just let me feed and walk him and I'll be ready to go."

"You know. I think I'm going to take Cornwallis. I'm going to put on his halter and styling plaid sweater," Paisley said.

"So, we're really doing this?" Bridget looked from face to face. They studied each other quietly.

Paisley broke the silence. "One for all."

"All for four," Sophie said.

Chapter Eighteen

Mashup

The road from the cove and the beach led up the green mountain. It was a clear but cold night. The rain forest was filled with old growth pines, ferns, and clovers the size of your hand. Trees blocked the waning sunlight and laid patterns of black shadow on the road.

Cars were parked end to end as far as Esther could see. "We're almost a mile away and I can hear the music. I bet we could hear it at your house."

"I hope it doesn't upset Spam. He's already in a new environment," Sophie said.

"What does he do when he's upset? You don't think he'll have an accident in the study, do you?" Paisley asked.

"No. He prefers to find shoes and pee in them."

"My poor Jimmys."

"Spam likes Berks."

There were no sidewalks, so they walked up the center of the road, stepping to the side as cars passed, dropped their passengers off, and turned around. Kids laughed, chattered, and greeted each other as they walked up the steep road until the trees opened into a parking lot.

Paisley stopped at the top of the road. "It's a good thing we walked. The closest parking space is a block away from the house." The music didn't stop. Grunge, Seattle Indy Rock, and Nirvana from the nineties played without a break.

"I don't hear a D.J. I don't know how we're going to sort out who is in charge. This is as good a turnout as we had for the Halloween haunted house," Sophie said.

"Jackson!" Bridget called and their friend Jackson turned and waved at her. He was surrounded by his new friends. A group of cosplay fans who met and reenacted scenes from Madison's books.

"There's Doctor Phelps," Esther said. The small hairs on the back of her neck rose. "He's with my neighbor, Marion. He has a ponytail. He fits the description, but he's a dad."

"Serial killers have been parents," Sophie said.

"There's Jax." Paisley pointed.

"Doctor Phelps is really nice and Jax is cool. I've been meeting with him planning the play almost daily, and I've never had any weird vibes," Bridget said.

"I hate to think of Jax being the son of a serial killer," Esther said.

"Maybe your creepy neighbor and Phelps are partners and Jax is actually thirty," Sophie said.

Esther laughed. She couldn't help it. As nervous as she was, Sophie could keep her laughing. "Keep your eyes open and be careful. We don't know who's listening."

Text from Parker. *I miss you.*

Esther replied, *I miss your face. *Smiley emoji, upside down smile emoji.**

Not a second passed. *I'm serious. I'm in a box with everything I thought I wanted and all I can think is, I wish you were here. I'm homesick for you. I don't want to ever be with anyone else but you.*

Esther's heart skipped a beat. She put her hand over her mouth to cover the massive smile that enveloped her face.

"E?" Sophie asked.

Esther held up a finger. She knew she had to answer. Somewhere he was standing with his phone, having laid his feelings out and waiting for an answer. But what to write, what to write?

Me more. Xoxoxoxo.

She erased all the x's and o's. Then she put one each. Then she hesitated.

Text from Parker: *R U there?*

E: *I am and I wish I was there.*

P: *Promise me you will stay home and stay safe tonight. I am so sorry I didn't go to* The End *with you. I can't stand the thought of you getting hurt. Please?*

She froze, starring at her phone. *Now what do I say?* She took a deep breath, blew it out slowly and typed rapidly with her thumbs.

E: *You know I am a cautious dork.*

P: *I can't stand this. Can I call when we get back to the hotel? It might be late?*

E: *Always.*

P: *Forever.*

Parker had never talked to Esther like this before. She didn't want to be at the Stone Circle. All she wanted was to be right where he was. Even if Simon's killer was never caught. Her entire soul ached for Parker until she realized Sophie had read the whole thing and was staring at her phone.

"Lock up your heart, E. We've got work to do." Sophie gave her a cheesy grin and rolled her eyes.

Esther held the phone to her chest for just a minute, hugging it, and then put it in her back pocket.

Some of the kids used their phones like flashlights. The points of light in the setting sun were spreading up the path and occasionally left it.

The trail emptied into the large clearing. The music thumped. "Where is the music coming from?" she yelled over the sound to Sophie.

Sophie pointed up in a nearby tree. An expensive name brand-speaker was somehow perched in the tree.

"I don't see any wires!" Esther said.

"Blue tooth!" Sophie pointed at several other speakers surrounding the clearing, including one in the stones.

Lights were also perched in various place. They were bright and at odd angles. The night sky turned scarlet and the clouds on the horizon were edged with gold as the sun moved behind them. The lights on the large Stonehenge replica cast dark shadows. The stage was well lit, but kids had glow bracelets and glow sticks.

"Sophie, look!" Ms. Priest's father, officer Neilson, was dressed in street clothes and standing by a large cardboard box of glow sticks. He greying hair was neatly combed but his mustache was still as shaggy as his overgrown eyebrows. Esther laughed. He was nodding his head and dancing just enough to make his tiny potbelly dance with the beat.

Paisley laughed loud enough that he heard her distinct laugh, his head snapped around, and his face turned pink.

Paisley leaned in closer so Esther, Sophie, and Bridget could hear her. "I can't tell who is in charge. I don't want to lie to my parents. I'm lousy at it. Let's go back and order our pizza."

Sophie nodded in agreement. "I want to check on Spam anyway."

Esther frowned. "I'm just going to do a walk around the perimeter of the party and make sure we aren't missing anything. I don't think we are, but just in case. Let's plan on coming up after the party to see who picks up the expensive speakers."

"I'll go with you," Bridget said.

"I don't think this loud music is good for Cornwallis, so we'll meet you back at the house with hot pizza." Paisley flashed her million-dollar smile and waved good-bye. She and Sophie melted into the crowd.

"Let's hurry." Esther stomach knotted. She felt half-dressed without Sophie. Like a bad dream where you find yourself at school in your underwear.

They started going to the right. The sun had set but there was still golden and red light reflected on the water. Kids stood on the edge of the grassy and rocky slope looking down thirty or forty feet to the beach below. They stopped for just a moment, taking it in. Logs and large stones littered the beach at the base of the cliff that was rarely traveled. When the tide came in, it tossed the logs around, making the beach a death trap. Someone got killed every year by logs rolling in the water.

Necanicum was almost a mile away, on the other side of the cove. Streetlamps on the promenade and sea wall started coming on one at a time. Esther thought it looked magical.

"Come on," Bridget said. They wove their way through friends and strangers, saying hello and trying not to be rude when they didn't stop.

Esther stopped again on the far side of the stones. "Nothing. Do you see anyone that looks like they are in charge?"

Esther spotted Mr. Mephisto sitting on a stone in the far corner of the terraced amphitheater. He looked like a dance chaperone irritated with the music. He was scanning the crowd and frowning.

Bridget shook her head, no. She looked around and stopped. She pointed at Officer Neilson and shrugged.

"I doubt he planned this," Esther smiled nervously. She knew Neilson. They became friends when he came to Madison's castle on the Washington Coast and arrested the real killer after he wrongfully accused her of killing an Oceanside High student.

Officer Neilson winked at her.

Why does everyone wink and why can't I? She closed both eyes and blinked rapidly. His brow furrowed and his left eye narrowed as if he was confused.

She realized Mephisto had watched the whole thing and gave her a counselor's smile of understanding that also said, I'm older and wiser than you are. She gave him a weak wave and half smile.

The stage was covered with kids dancing, laughing, and playing. Kids were everywhere.

Then Esther felt something under her feet, vertigo, birds flew in the dark, and she heard the sound of a freight train. No, it can't be? An airplane? Bridget's nails dug into her arm.

The music still thumped but phones went off everywhere, it was like watching a terrifying game of phone tag.

It was a tsunami warning.

Kids began screaming and running. Someone thankfully climbed a tree and shut one of the speakers off. Then they turned off the others one by one or they fell out of the trees and shattered until only one was left.

Neilson passed her. He looked at her, like he was sick. "I have to get to the station before traffic bottlenecks!" He was moving faster than she had ever seen him move.

"Esther! Esther!"

Her heart was racing, and the chaos was so loud, when the last speaker went silent, she realized Bridget was screaming her name and was trying to pull her the opposite way of the crowd. Of course.

"Stop! Up! Stop! Up the mountain!" She screamed at the backs of panicked friends she'd known most of her life. No one stopped.

"Come on!" Bridget yelled.

Esther looked up the mountain. They weren't by the trail. They would have to go down to the parking lot to find it. They would be running into the woods in the dark.

"Maybe we are high enough?" Esther said. Her phone vibrated. It blew up. Bridget looked at hers.

Parker. *We all got the text warning. We are on our way home as fast as we can get out of the stadium.*

Mom. *We got the warning. We are trying to come down the mountain to meet you. Drive to the junction. If you can't drive—run! Go up, Esther. Go up! We will find you. Where are you.*

Esther texted two words back to her mother. *The End.*

Her mother didn't respond. Esther couldn't wait. "Up, Bridget!" Bridget nodded.

Sirens went off loud and long. It sounded like a World War II air-raid. Esther hesitated.

Text from Sophie. *We're running. Go up the mountain. Getting Spam. We will find you.*

A second later she got a text from Paisley: *They are closing all the roads. No one can get in. No parents. Bunker! Spotty service. Meet at bunker!*

A jolt went through Esther. The bunker was where a stalker had taken Paisley last summer. Miss Molly was home alone. She would be so afraid. Jumbled thoughts, dark memories, and a driving need to run for her life pushed her on.

Esther was running in the dark. Bridget had let go of her arm and was ahead of her. It was so much darker without the kids and the lights. She stumbled and looked back at the city. Car headlights popped on like someone had flipped a switch. Mesmerized, she watched them move toward the mountain and stop.

The siren stopped and a man's voice came on. "This is not a drill." Then the sirens began again. She turned to run and couldn't see Bridget.

"Bridget!" Esther screamed. She was drowned out by the sirens.

A coast guard helicopter flew over the mountain shining a spotlight on the ground. A voice from the helicopter broadcast a desperate message. "This is not a drill. Get to high ground. This is not a drill."

Esther waited for their light so she could get a good look at where she was going and maybe see Bridget. The light shone on her. The voice bellowed, "Get to high ground! This is not a drill."

She turned to run and bathed in the spotlight stood Mr. Mephisto.

"Mr. Mephisto! Follow me! We have to get to higher ground." The ground vibrated and Esther thought she saw it roll. He smiled at her and followed her into the woods.

She could still hear the sirens as she picked her way through the woods in the dark, with only the moon and stars to light her way. She couldn't run fast enough.

"Here," Mephisto held up his phone as a flashlight.

"Save your battery! We might need it!" she yelled over the noise.

He shut the light off, but it had temporarily blinded her. She paused, rubbed her eyes and waited for it to pass.

"Come on." She motioned for him to follow.

"Don't worry, Bella. Everything is going to be okay."

Bella? A mistake—she didn't correct him. They left the clearing and had to climb over a large fallen tree. The going was slower. Some kids must have gone this way. She could hear them further up the mountain screaming. She hoped she would find Bridget.

"Bridget!" she screamed. "Bridget!"

"Esther!" Bridget called from just a little to the left, up the mountain. She shifted her direction.

Something caught her braid and yanked her back. She lost her footing and fell hard, catching herself with her hand, cutting it on a stick. She reached back to get her hair loose from the branch that must have caught it and felt hands.

"That's the wrong way, Bella. Our picnic is that way."

"Mr. Mephisto! It's Esther! We have to go up!"

"I didn't want to tell you. I wanted to surprise you. I love our secret times together at the falls."

Mephisto was speaking, but whatever he saw—existed between his own ears. Esther remembered what her mother had taught her class during one of her sexual assault prevention lectures.

"Mr. Mephisto. Look at me! I'm Esther. You're in Necanicum. I am not Bella."

He bared his teeth and growled. His eyes were void of light. "I know you don't mean it. Let's not play that game, Bella." He yanked her braid back and she cried out in pain.

She heard the helicopter coming back their way. Maybe if I can get their attention. The spotlight moved above, coming closer. He started dragging her by her braided ponytail. She clung onto his arm, spinning, desperately trying to get her feet under her. She stumbled and caught herself with her hands again on the rocks.

The light moved closer. He yanked her under the bows of a large pine tree and put a knife to her throat. The ground under the trees was protected and moist, slippery.

"I love hiding with you, Bella. Our parents will never find us here." He smiled at someone else while looking at her with his soulless eyes.

"Mr. Mephisto!"

He pulled her closer to him and used one arm to pin her against his chest with the knife in view and the other to hold her braid so tightly she felt her skin pulling loose. She stumbled but tried to walk ahead of him while her mind raced.

Her phone vibrated in her pocket, against his leg. He picked it out of her back pocket and threw it. She felt hope go with it.

They stumbled, walked, and then climbed through the underbrush on what looked like an elk or deer trail. It was narrow in the moonlight, and often disappeared altogether. Within a few minutes the trail opened into a clearing.

A gushing waterfall reflected the moonlight. Esther didn't know where they were, but she knew by the dark, still color of the pond at the base that it was deep enough to drown in. Surrounded by rocks, ground cover, and tiny flowers, it would have been beautiful if she didn't have a knife at her throat.

A picnic basket and blanket were neatly laid out by the pond. A solar lantern was bright enough for her to see that there was food in the basket and drinks.

I have to be smart. I have to play along so he lets go of me. "What's your first name?"

"You know. You're teasing me. Everyone does. Only war criminals spell Josef, with an f. I don't know what my father was thinking."

"Tell me about your father."

"He hated everything. He's gone now. Good riddance. He didn't like you, but I love you. I always will. We will be together forever."

Almost the same words Parker had used just minutes earlier, but these felt like he was threatening her life. *Play along!* Her mother's voice ran through her mind.

"How was school today?" Esther said.

He beamed and held her tighter, but the knife wasn't as close to her face as it had been.

"It was okay. It's better now that I am here with you. Who did you let braid your hair? You know I love braiding your hair."

"I tried to do it myself. That's why it looks so bad. Did you plan the party? *The End?*"

"Sweet, sweet, Bella. I knew if we met at a party again—we could have our picnic. You were my first love, Bella. I remember on our first date the way you laughed. I knew you would be mine forever. We had two-hundred and sixty-three sunrises and sunsets together by our waterfall. I would braid your hair for you as the sun set. You shouldn't have tried to leave me."

He swung her around to face the basket. "Look, I made your favorite. You don't ever need to worry. I will always keep you close to me."

Bile rose in her stomach. "It's me! It's Esther, Mr. Mephisto! I'm not Bella." She struggled, she kicked back at his legs, she tried to free herself, the way her mother had taught her. She pushed on the inside of his elbow and began trying to push his arm off of her airways and the knife away from her neck. She pushed with everything she was worth. He was strong and yanked her braid so far back she fell onto the blanket on her back. She rolled over and tried to crawl away.

He put his knee in her back and pulled zip ties out of the basket, tying her hands behind her back. He was rough when he sat her up again.

The sirens wailed, but they sounded more distant. The helicopter continued to warn residents, flying away and then back to the nearby park. Esther couldn't hear anyone else. She was on her own.

"Why did you feed Sophie bad donuts?"

"I knew she would get in the way of our special picnic time." He frowned and sat her up. Then he smiled as if he remembered something. "I didn't get sick. I only put arsenic on her donut."

She remembered her mother saying keep the perpetrator talking and look for a way out. Even if you have to tell them how wonderful they are. "Then why did you break into her house?"

"She took my photo from Simon's hand. You're too sweet. I knew you would never betray me, but she is vitriol, a snake in the garden. I had to get that photo back. What if she had picked up more? I went to find her walking her dog, like all the nights I watched her. If she was out of the way, we could be together without her snarky, little mouth.

"When I got into the house, I couldn't find the photo. But while I looked, I had a brilliant idea. Something only I would think of. I planted the seed to clear the way for our love. I logged into a computer as the host of *The End*. Genius really." His self-satisfied laugh made her skin crawl. "I made it look like she was a student who wanted to kill a fellow student. Tomorrow, after our moment, I will make a report to law enforcement that she is dangerous to herself and others. They will put her on a 72-hour hold in a mental institution based on my word. Then they will find her login to *The End* at home and the psych hold will become permanent. She won't interfere with our time together, ever again."

"You planned this using borrowed computers like hers?"

"I started on Simon's computer while I stayed with him. Your computer is nicer and so is your cat. I couldn't wait to see the look of joy on your face when we were finally together."

Her heart was beating so loud, she was breathless. It was hard to talk.

"Is that why you killed Simon? To make sure we had our time together? So, he wouldn't interfere with us?"

"That was Simon's fault. He had Bob work on his computer for free. Bob found a cache of my favorite photos on Simon's home computer and realized I was behind the event. He had to go before he spoiled our time together. I have been thinking and dreaming about this for months."

Esther spotted something in the bushes to their right. She glanced without turning her head. He babbled on about love, while she watched the outline of what she hoped was Bridget hiding behind the base of a tree only twelve feet away. Maybe she had called for help. Not that anyone could get there. The roads would be clogged with traffic, if it was like the tsunami warning in 2011. The 2011 tsunami was used by the teachers to scare students into compliance when they ran drills.

Bridget inched closer and slid to the next tree. Esther mouthed the word *no*, but realized it was too dark, Bridget couldn't see her lips.

Esther tried to distract him. "After lunch, what did you have in mind?"

He laughed a deep throaty laugh.

The sirens wailed. "This is not a drill." The helicopter was coming. Bridget would be exposed if the light hit her. She had to distract him so he wouldn't see Bridget.

"I'm so hungry. Did you bring my favorite?"

"Oh, my darling Bella. I will always remember your favorite. I have a whole box of cherry chocolates. Would you like one now?"

The spotlight swept the forest. In the distance she could hear some kids shouting. Thankfully they were climbing the steep mountain.

Her mind raced while it felt like time stood still. She knew what to do. She had to buy time and protect Bridget, but how. She had an idea. The awfulness of it sunk in even as she executed her plan.

She pushed back gently on his stomach, so the knife was further away and then, acting, and hopefully nailing the part, she relaxed her muscles, stopped fighting, and spoke to him in a soft, sultry voice. "You were wise to kill Simon. I took the photo out of his hand. I had to protect you and our time together." She turned, her neck strained, and smiled. "Braid my hair, Josef."

He dropped the knife and ran to the basket while she worked to get onto her knees. She didn't get a chance. He was back too soon.

He dropped to his knees behind her and undid her hair. Disgusted, she shivered as he began brushing it.

Hypervigilant, she heard another sound. It was Cornwallis. Bridget stepped back and Esther lost her in the shadows. Frantically, she scanned the woods.

He spoke loudly over the chaos. "Do you remember our first picnic? Of course, you do. We will never forget it. I will always keep mementoes of our time together, precious." He gently brushed her hair, sending shivers up and down her spine.

Then Esther did something she hadn't done in a while. She closed her eyes and prayed.

The helicopter made another sweep. There were two now. Another had joined in the distance. When they left the mountain to sweep their lights across the beach and ocean, she heard barking again, mixed with the bone chilling sound of the sirens. "This is not a drill. This is not a drill," and back to the sound of fear—sirens, mixed with screams in the distance.

She took a deep breath. The words came to her like someone else was saying them. "My love? My hands are going numb. I want to be free." She looked up at his face. His head snapped up and his eyes met hers. He picked up the knife and cut the zip ties.

The barking was distant. She had to buy time. She reached up and touched his disgusting face. *I'm going to be sick.* He jolted and she thought he was going to drop the brush. Then she heard it clearly. Barking between rounds of the siren and the helicopter.

In a split second his head turned, a flash of fur burst out of the bushes and tiny Spam latched himself to Mephisto's ankle, while Cornwallis had his arm. Esther scrambled to her feet.

Everything was crystal clear and slow motion. He kicked and poor Spam's tiny body skittered across the clearing. She scooped up Spam and looked over her shoulder for Cornwallis. He had Mephisto's arm and was shaking it while he struggled to get to the knife.

She ran for all she was worth, slipping, tumbling, into Paisley's arms, pulled by Sophie, pushed by Bridget. They fell as much as they ran down the mountain.

A yelp from behind them made Paisley freeze and they ran into her back. She turned and looked up the trail, her mouth open, her eyes wide with terror.

There was nothing they could do. They had to keep running.

The trees gave way to the Stone Circle, an ominous silhouette. The ground rumbled again, the sirens wailed and the world looked like the nightmares of war. All the headlights stopped in the distance. She knew people would be running and struggling for high ground. A sob caught in her throat, but she couldn't stop.

"We can't go down!" Sophie screamed. They scrambled up the rise to the middle of the stones and Sophie climbed on the alter in the center. Wind mixed with rain made her hair stand out in a wild mess against the backdrop of a full-blown storm on the ocean.

Sophie reached down and took Spam's shivering body from her arms. Climbing with the girls to stand on the stones, they watched in horror and fascination.

And then it happened. The ocean pulled back and when it receded, it exposed stones, logs, and the rolling sand beneath what had always been hidden by waves. They held each other's hands.

"We have to run!" Esther shouted. They climbed off the rock. They couldn't predict how high the water would be when it returned. They were only thirty or forty feet above sea level.

"He's coming!" Bridget screamed.

The helicopter spotlight stopped overhead, lighting the way for Cornwallis who was running toward them like mighty lion.

Behind Cornwallis, Mephisto burst through the trees, knife held in the air. And then like a scene from a movie, the heroes arrived.

Esther's mother burst through the trees with Mrs. Stuart and Madison. Mephisto stopped, he froze for a split second, his perfect hair whipping in the wind. He looked at Esther and kept coming.

"Run!" Esther screamed and pointed at high ground. The girls took off without looking back. Esther went the other way and Mephisto followed. The mothers followed him.

Esther ran for all she was worth. She came closer and closer to the cliff's edge. She glanced back, just in time to see her mother fly through the air like a crazed animal and land on Mephisto's back, smoothly taking him in a choke hold and twisting until he fell to the ground. He tried to roll over, but she rode him, her crazy, curly hair wild in the wind, while Madison and Mrs. Stuart kicked the living stuffing out of him and Cornwallis chewed on his leg.

Then like the psychotic serial killer he was, he rose from the pile and swiped the knife in a broad circle. Melissa Stuart took Cornwallis's collar and held him back. In the chaos, Sophie and the girls had turned around and were running toward them.

Mephisto looked at her with a maniacal smile, knife held high, and ran in her direction. But the mothers were hot on his heels screaming and the copter was hovering nearby.

A cable dropped from the helicopter between Mephisto and Esther. He ran past it and then he passed her as a Coast Guard rescue diver slid to the ground.

The man shouted a command. Esther only caught one word in the wind, "Stop!" The seaman ran fearlessly toward the knife and Mephisto.

Mephisto only stopped for a second and looked at Esther from the cliff's edge. The wind whipped his words away. He smiled and went over the edge, slipping and sliding to the rocks below.

Esther ran to the edge. He was still alive, sliding and rolling down the rocky embankment. The helicopter moved overhead and kept the spotlight on him. He climbed over logs and in only a minute began running the dry bed of the ocean across the cove toward town. The spotlight followed. The siren's warned without knowing the real danger had been at school with the children the entire time. Rain pelted her face, and the wind whipped her hair.

The mothers and Cornwallis ran to Esther's side and watched in horror as the water began to come back. Her mother gathered her in her arms, wet hair everywhere.

"Where is Grandma and Mary?" Esther said.

"Still at the restaurant on the mountain!"

Satisfied they were safe, Esther held Sophie's hand and leaned against her mother while they watched like a united front of terrifying strength. The water, sounding like a freight train, roared back in over Mephisto.

Violent waves kept coming. In unison, they turned and ran screaming, following the seaman through the stones, across the park, up the seats to the highest spot they could reach.

The seaman began running up through the trees with everyone following him. Esther stopped and held her breath, watching the roaring ocean in the light of the helicopter.

The first wave crashed against the cliff, shooting white foam ten feet in the air behind Stonehenge. She knew it wouldn't be the only wave and so she climbed on.

They had made it to higher ground and watched a safe distance from the cliffs, hundreds of feet above the ocean.

Wave after wave had engulfed the lighthouse on the rook. They thought it was over when the seaman who was in contact with the helicopter by radio said there would be a second set of waves—and there was.

A new roaring series of violent waves crashed against the beach below over and over again until the sirens stopped, and the water calmed, as if it were any other rainy evening.

"Ma'am. I've been given the all-clear. You're safe to make your way carefully back down the mountain." The rugged young man smiled, his teeth white in the evening light.

"Aren't you escorting us?" Madison said. "What if he survived?"

"I doubt that very much, ma'am. But if he did, I'm sure you could handle him. Excuse me, but I am taking the chopper home." The line dropped, he hooked up and they flew away while still hoisting him into the orange and white helicopter.

"Where are we?" Paisley asked.

"Home." Esther laughed. "Mom and I can lead you down. We hike this mountain every year."

"Let's go east until we meet the main trail. We should watch for other kids," her mother said.

"Caw, caw!" Sophie called out.

"Caw, caw!" Esther answered.

"Caw, caw!" Mrs. Stuart said, and giggled.

For almost an hour they called to each other while hiking back to the parking lot at the Stone Circle.

"Where did you park, Mom?" Bridget asked Madison.

"On the Countz family lawn on this side of the river." Madison shrugged.

"How did you get here so fast? The restaurant is ten miles away and I'm sure the roads were closed," Esther said.

"You should have seen her," Mrs. Stuart said.

"What is the point in having an expensive SUV if you don't off-road with it?" And we were going against traffic. Everyone was trying to leave, and we were trying to get to you, once Sophie told us where you were."

"Your mother was a road warrior. We're going to have to apologize to the golf course owner, Ironpot, and that nice state trooper." Mrs. Stuart laughed and gave Madison a buddy hug. "I'll pitch in on the landscaping and help if you're assigned community service."

"What impressed me was our run," Esther's mom said. "Our training paid off."

Madison looked at Esther. "Honey, never get between a mother and her baby, just ask your mom."

"Ow." Esther's mom smiled. "I'm sorry. I don't know what came over me."

"You were a warrior, Mrs. J! Isn't that right, Spam?" Sophie said. Spam panted in her arms.

Grace smiled. "I'm seriously embarrassed. When some people get scared, they run, or they freeze, and sometimes they fight. I have a third setting, Mom goes nuclear."

Cars were scattered and parked all over the streets and even on some sidewalks. The drivers who had abandoned them were making their way off the east hill and weaving through the apocalyptic scene. Other drivers idled, waiting for the cars blocking their way to move. It would be hours before the roads were totally cleared.

The highest waves had sent logs like javelins across the road above the cove. "Look at my scanner feed," Sophie said. "See over there? The scanner group has video of that log running the vacation rental through." The massive piece of driftwood stuck out of a second story window. Large boulders were scattered on the road and on top of an abandoned economy car.

Esther stopped in the parking lot of the cove. From here she could see the entire length of the beach. The old-fashioned streetlamps lit up the sea wall and promenade. Spotlights at the turnaround were pointed onto the beach. There was a lot of noise on the mountain. She could hear traffic, but nothing on the ocean side of town was moving.

The ocean rolled in and out, the pulse of their little town.

"Look at the beach," Esther said. Then she realized they were all looking at the beach. "It's amazing. It must have come right up to the sea wall, like the tsunami in 1964." The sand had been washed into new and different dunes with large pieces of driftwood and even piles of rock moved up against the sea wall.

"Do you think Mr. Mephisto made it?" Paisley looked at Esther.

Paisley's mom put her arm around Paisley and shook her head. "It's not likely."

Esther's mother moved to a higher vantage point on a rock. "Do you think our house is okay? I can't tell from here if the wave went over the wall."

"I'm searching the scanner group," Sophie said. "I've found it to be a very reliable resource, if not entertaining. Okay, here it is. Harvey Bart, the group's moderator, is asking everyone to comment on damage in the same thread. He says, and the thread seems to agree— or at least the last five comments—that there is no major damage in town other than the cove. Waller City, further down the coast has some flooding, but not as bad as 1964. The dock at the old cannery is damaged. Oh, but Agnes Fuller says it had dry rot anyway." Sophie smiled. "Look, our security cameras caught the waves from the beach side of our street."

Sophie held up her phone. Everyone crowded around her. "Whoa, look at that log. The water got close, but didn't reach our house, which means the others on our street and behind the seawall are probably fine. I wonder if your new neighbor knew what to do when the alarms went off. Has he lived by the ocean before?"

"He came from Arizona," Esther said. "He's an inlander. We should have told him what to do. Poor guy was probably stuck rounding his cats up."

"Well, I'm amazed it didn't just go from this parking lot right into the Captain's House," Mrs. Stuart said.

"The house has been standing for over a hundred years." Madison smiled and gave her a little hug. "Of course, it's fine."

Esther's mom sighed. "Then, I had better be getting your Grandma Mable from the restaurant. She's probably frustrated. I'm surprised she hasn't called us yet. You picked me up, Madison, so I need to ride with you. We need to get your car off the Countz's lawn and leave them a note about their sprinkler head."

"Here's Grandma Mable," Sophie said. She passed her phone to Esther's mom. "Someone caught her on the scanner page. You know how everyone always evacuates to the Train Station Restaurant Parking lot? Somebody brought their Karaoke Machine!" Sophie laughed and turned the phone towards Esther. "Someone's got your grandma on live feed singing Staying Alive with Mary and your neighbor, Marion, in the back of a pickup truck. Isn't that Doctor Phelps? Look!"

Esther was afraid. She took the phone from Sophie's hand. There Grandma Mable was in all her glory doing her favorite rendition of the Bee Gees 1977 hit song from Saturday Night Fever.

"Well, you can tell by the way I . . ."

Esther groaned and then couldn't help it, she was laughing. "They're doing the shake your booty dance." She handed the phone to her mom.

"We're too late to save her," her mom said. "That's what I get for leaving Mom alone."

"No wonder Marion likes her," Sophie said. "She's a Bee Gees fan with a wiggle."

"I hope no one at work saw this." Esther's mother handed the phone back to Sophie.

Sophie scrolled a little. "Don't you work with a Joan Anderson?"

"Yes," Esther's mom said.

"Too late. She saw it. She says she loves your mom." Sophie giggled.

"I feel weird without my phone," Esther said. "Has anyone heard from Parker?"

As if he read her mind, Paisley's phone rang and so did Mrs. Stuarts's, and her mothers.

"It's for you." Paisley gave Esther her phone.

"Parker, where are you? I am so sorry I didn't text earlier. I lost my phone. You didn't have to miss the game for me."

"We were all afraid we would lose you. Nothing, not even football, was more important than getting back to you and making sure you're all safe. I know I've been kind of cheap and lazy lately. I'll never take us for granted again. I love you, Esther, and I think I always will."

There were those three words she was dying to hear. Doubt and fear crept up from her gut and she realized she was shivering. *Say something!*

"I love you too." She stopped walking for a minute and listened. When he didn't say anything, she went on. "There is nothing to forgive, but if there was, I would forget it in a minute. I learned something else today. Life is precious. Hanging onto the past can turn you into a sad serial killer. I think I am finally ready to work on forgiving my dad. You were right. My anger only hurts me."

"That's what I love about you. You constantly change, your heart is beautiful, and your courage is amazing," Parker said.

Sophie elbowed her and made a kissy face. Esther laughed. Sophie took the phone out of Esther's hand. "She lost her phone. We're going to your house. Are you close? I see." She hung up. "I'm starving. We're going to need more pizza. Do you think they're delivering?"

They continued making their way home through the giant parking lot.

Chapter Nineteen

Clickbait

It was one thing to air kiss in the run-through, but it was quite another to really kiss Jax in the play, while Parker looked on. Out of the corner of her eye, she could see Parker, who was in charge of lights and sound, frowning with his arms folded. Nephi was on a tall ladder with a giant sifter of potato flakes for the final magical scene. Bob had a firm grip on Nephi's ladder. No one else was going down on his watch.

"Go, Esther, go," Doctor Phelps whispered. She realized it was her line. She strode on stage, which was difficult in her white velvet gown and heavy red velvet cape. Nephi shook potato snow in clumps onto the stage making the audience giggle.

Jax, who looked fine in his tights and medieval costume leapt to his feet and fell prostrate at hers. "My fairy princess. Do not become a godmother. Stay with me! Marry me." He held out a garish plastic ring.

She held out her hand. Jax slipped the ring on. Parker folded his arms and scowled. *What if I like the kiss? What if Parker can tell I think Jax is gorgeous?* She felt her heart rate pickup and her cheeks caught fire.

"We will never be parted again." Esther projected her voice to the crowd, but her eyes were on Parker. Jax took her in his arms and kissed her. It was long and slobbery.

Nothing. I feel nothing. Not like Parker. He's white lightning.

The lights went out and she scurried off stage holding onto Jax in the dark. She jumped off the side and practically into Parker's waiting arms.

A single spotlight switched on and focused on Bridget, sitting alone with her guitar on the edge of the stage. Esther knew her well enough to know that she was terrified and hadn't eaten much for days because her anxiety about this moment was so bad. Madison was on the opposite side of the stage from Esther. She had her hands clasped at her heart, waiting.

Because Bridget sat silently, the curious audience quieted and focused entirely on her. Esther had heard the piece Bridget had written a hundred times now. But that was okay. It had become a favorite.

I'll stand by your side when the stars fall from heaven.
I'll hold your hand when the moon turns to blood.
And when the night forgets to come,
I will run straight to you.

Bridget's voice was as beautiful and rich as any singer Esther had ever heard. After she performed the first verse flawlessly, a single male voice came from the woods.

It was rich like cream and butter. A smooth tenor stepped into the second spotlight. Jax sang his verse, while he walked to the stage.

She stood by him, and they looked at each other and sang the first verses like a round, followed by the chorus again in unison.

I'll stand by your side when the stars fall from heaven.
I'll hold your hand when the moon turns to blood.
And when the night forgets to come,
I will run straight to you.

The audience jumped to their feet wildly applauding and waving a flame on their cell phones, like a hundred twinkle lights in the night sky.

Startled, Esther felt Parker wrap his arms around her from behind and kiss her neck. "I'll stand by your side until the stars fall from heaven."

She turned and held him close.

"Well, enough of that mush," Parker said. "It's time to clean up this mess and take this show on the road."

Confused, Esther stood still with her mouth open while Parker and Nephi began frantically cleaning up with the help of their parents. She didn't know what to say. So, she took off her cape and gently folded it into its cardboard box. She pulled the gown over her head, careful not to let her t-shirt go with it, and she rolled down the legs of her jeans before putting the gown in the same box. Dislodging the tiara from her curly hair was a bit more difficult.

"Are you ready?" Sophie said. She held up Spam so Esther could pet him. "It's time to feed Spam."

"Shouldn't we help clean up?"

"Look around, E. It's almost done, and Doctor Phelps says the potato flakes will go away during the next wind or rainstorm." She hugged Spam.

She was right. Nephi came jogging by on one end of the ladder and Bob was trying to keep up on the other end.

"What is going on?" Esther asked. "We never clean anything up this fast."

Sophie yawned and shrugged.

Parker jumped on the clean stage in the completely cleared Stone Circle Park. "Follow Me!" He waved toward the parking lot and as if he were the Pied Piper, they followed quietly down the trail.

Parker jogged to catch up to Esther. He flashed a goofy grin and squeezed her hand before jogging on ahead. Esther and Sophie plodded on.

Just as she entered the clearing she heard, "Meep, Meep." Car dome lights came on and Parker waved joyfully from the driver's seat in his VW van like a boy riding his first bike.

"Road trip!" he yelled. Nephi passed Esther and pulled open the side door. The van was full of supplies and their surf boards were tied on top. Paisley and Bridget got in and were happily chatting.

Another car honked and she realized her mom and Papa J had boards on their SUV and were idling behind the van. Mary was waving her wand out the back window. Grandma Mable gave her the hang loose hand signal.

Her smiling mother leaned out the window. "Didn't see the mystery van coming, did you?"

Papa J waved. "You've got more to learn, super sleuth!"

Esther started laughing. She snorted and then Sophie started laughing. It was infectious.

Madison and the Stuarts were behind Papa J's SUV.

The little convoy pulled out with Esther in the front seat, watching Parker grind the gears and learn to use the stick shift. At the first stop sign, he turned on a small speaker, taped to the dash.

A local Indie band's music poured out of the speakers and Esther put her head and arms out of the window and screamed, "Woo Hoo!" They all cheered and howled at the full moon as the van chugged down highway 101.

The End . . . or is it?

About the Author

© Photo by Haley Miller Captures

Shannon Symonds writes in an old house by the sea, where her six children, their children, and thirty or forty of her closest relatives and their dogs come and go constantly. She loves laughter, a good mystery, running on the beach, deep sea fishing, and bonfires. Her all-time favorite job at church was girls' camp activity director.

Shannon worked for over twenty years as an advocate serving survivors of abuse alongside law enforcement, as a home visitor supporting new mothers, and on other causes she is ridiculously passionate about. She will tell you, "Love sprinkled with laughter really is the answer. It always was, and it always will be."

Scan to visit

https://www.cozymysteriesbythesea.com/